AF282592

Vincent J. Staude

Anniversary

Imprint

Bibliographic information of the German National Library: The German National Library lists this publication in the German National Bibliography; detailed bibliographic data are available on the Internet at http://dnb.dnb.de.

© 2023 Vincent J. Staude

Production and publisher: BoD - Books on Demand, Norderstedt

ISBN: 978-3-7583-1927-3

Main persons

Tung Ming Wah – Detective with the Narcotics Bureau HKPF, later Inspector with the Metropolitan Police, London.

Chow Nie Wen – Best friend and former partner of Tung Ming Wah at Narcotics Bureau HKPF; private investigator

Wong Wei Yan – Son of Wong Zhao Wen, Chairman of Yi Wong

Robert Duncan – Englishman, best friend of Wong Wei Yan

Other persons involved

LONDON

Superintendent Alcott – Tung Ming Wah's superior in the Metropolitan Police, London.

Peter Johnson – Metropolitan Police, Photofit Specialist

Fat Liu – Informant in London

Charles Buchanan – Inspector, leads investigation regarding the abduction of Tung Ai Mui

Alison Blair – Half-sister of Robert Duncan, girlfriend of Wong Wei Yan

HONG KONG

Tung Ai Ling – Wife of Tung Ming Wah

Tung Ai Mui – Daughter of Tung Ming Wah, call name: Mui

Superintendent Lau – Superintendent of Narcotics Bureau HKPF

Wong Zhao Wen – Chairman of Yi Wong, father of Wong Wei Yan and Chow Nie Wen

Inspector Cheung – Leads the HK investigation team regarding the abduction case of Tung Ai Mui

Officer Cheng – HK Abduction Investigation Team

Officer Mary Lee – HK Abduction Investigation Team

"Keung" – HK Abduction Investigation Team

"Sam" – HK Abduction Investigation Team

"Ming" – HK Abduction Investigation Team

Johnny Lee – Police Informant in HK

Inspector Choi – Inspector investigating the HK Homicide

Chan Mei Ling – Assistant to Inspector Cheung

Kwong Wai Ming – Confidant of Wong Zhao Wen, advisor of Wong Wei Yan

2 July 1998, 22:37, Hong Kong Island

Superintendent Lau had ordered the team into the meeting room. When he quickly entered the room, they were already sitting around the large meeting table.

"Can anyone of you explain to me what went wrong earlier?" he bellowed into the round as he threw a thick file onto the table with a loud bang.

He put both fists at his sides. His eyes met concerned faces. He looked at them in turn, sitting at the table, tired and disappointed.

"As far as I remember, the handover and therefore the arrest was scheduled for Friday."

Pause.

"Is it Friday today?"

Some shook their heads, avoiding any eye contact with the Superintendent.

"Why, pray, was the arrest brought forward then? - And look at me!"

Tung Ming Wah stood up.

"Because I ordered it."

Superintendent Lau looked at him angrily. Today had not been the best day. And his mood was particularly bad.

"I got information at short notice that the transaction had been brought forward." Wah defended his decision.

"Why wasn't I informed?" the Superintendent snapped at him.

Mei tentatively raised her hand.

"You had a lunch appointment, sir," she said quietly.

His head snapped over to her, she quickly put her hand down.

"Usually that doesn't stop you from calling me about every little thing."

"But this time you said you didn't want to be disturbed," Mei replied meekly.

"Sir, I alone bear full responsibility." Wah remarked, drawing the Superintendent's attention back to himself.

He had been investigating the Yi Wong syndicate for months.

"Yes, damn you! You do!" the Superintendent shouted and hit the table with the flat of his hand.

"And now I would like to know what happened out there! How can it be that Wong Zhao Wen, the Chairman of Yi Wong himself, is the only one to be shot! That's nineteen months of work nothing down the drain. For nothing!"

Wah looked at the floor. In his opinion, the statement of the last sentence was somewhat exaggerated. After all, they had seized fifty-eight kilograms of Heroin No. 4, arrested seven gang members of the Thai drug trafficker and ten members of the Yi Wong syndicate.

There was a knock at the door.

"What's wrong, Keung?" Superintendent Lau gave his assistant who had just entered an angry look.

"Sir, would you please come to your office?" he replied calmly.

The Superintendent looked around once more and left the room. When he closed the door behind him, everyone breathed a sigh of relief and relaxed a little.

"What is it?" asked the Superintendent irritably.

"Inspector Choi from the homicide department would like to speak to you."

"What does he want?"

Keung shrugged his shoulders.

"I don't know what it's about. But it seems serious."

"I'll be right there."

He pressed his lips together and went back into the meeting room.

"The meeting is over for today. Wah, you wait in your office. The rest of you can go."

With these words, he picked up the file he had thrown on the table earlier and left the room.

Most of them were glad not to be in Wah's position. He was in charge of the operation and now had to answer questions.

"Good night." said Wah, "Thank you for your hard work."

He tried to cheer up his colleagues a little. They had done their best, after all, and although the arrest had gone wrong, they had dealt a bitter blow to the syndicate. Chow Nie Wen walked towards Wah.

"What's wrong with him?"

"I don't know. But I'm sure I'll find out sooner than I'd like," Wah replied.

Nie Wen patted Wah briefly on the shoulder and grinned.

"I'll stick around. Maybe we can go for a drink after the Superintendent ripped your head off."

"If I do that, Ai Ling will definitely rip my head off. - But she'll probably do that anyway: it's our wedding anniversary today and I stood her up at the restaurant. Believe me, right now she's clearly the bigger danger than the Superintendent," Wah replied, playfully contrite.

"Then don't forget to get a Taoist incantation on your way home so you can stick the note on her forehead before her evil spirit can harm you," Nie Wen countered.

Wah started laughing out loud.

"I already have it in the drawer. Red ink on yellow paper, as it should be." Wah snorted.

Nie Wen grinned mischievously to himself as he walked to his desk.

Wah closed his office door and looked at the desk with a sigh. The papers were piling up. He still had some reports to write and the internal investigations regarding the death of Wong Zhao Wen would start soon. He sat down in his chair and looked out the window. How beautiful Hong Kong was. Especially at night. Partially he could look out over Victoria Harbour and see the tourist ships with their festive lights. Sighing, he turned back to his desk and his eyes fell on the framed picture that stood next to the screen. A beautiful Chinese woman and a little girl with two pigtails sticking up smiled at him. Actually, he should have been home at this time.

If it hadn't been for the early arrest, he would have met Ai Ling in the restaurant. It was their seventh wedding anniversary. Their little daughter Ai Mui was spending the night with her grandparents. It would have been a nice evening. Wah took the small package out of his desk drawer and opened it. The necklace with the diamond pendant would surely please Ai Ling. 'Hopefully it will make it a little easier for her to forgive me for the messed up wedding anniversary.' he thought with a smile. He could imagine how beautiful this necklace would look on Ai Ling's neck. Tomorrow morning he would prepare a special breakfast for her and then present her with the gift.

The department had become quiet. Most of the colleagues had gone home. Nie Wen and three other colleagues sat at their desks and worked away. Again and again they glanced at the Superintendent's office. A visitor sat with his back to the glass door. The Superintendent hardly spoke. But he shook his head incessantly and had his mouth covered with a hand. What was it about? What was the visitor telling him?

Twenty minutes later, they shook hands silently and the visitor left the Superintendent's office. The Superintendent immediately walked towards Wah's office. He looked tired.

Wah looked up from the files as the Superintendent quietly closed the door behind him. His expression did not bode well. The Superintendent did not say a word. He walked to the blinds on the office windows and turned them closed. Wah watched him quietly. When all the blinds were closed, the Superintendent sat down on the visitor's chair in front of Wah's desk.

"I had a visit from Inspector Choi of Homicide."

Wah looked at him in amazement.

"What has homicide got to do with it?" asked Wah in astonishment.

"It wasn't about our case," replied Superintendent Lau. "There was an attack with a car bomb in Wan Chai. He was here because he had some information for us."

Wah drew his eyebrows together.

"What do we have to do with attacks? We are the Narcotics Bureau."

Superintendent Lau shook his head and looked down. Wah sensed that something bad must have happened. He had never seen the Superintendent like this before. Wah leaned forward.

"What's wrong?" he asked insistently.

"It was your car." the Superintendent replied slowly.

"Beg your pardon?"

Wah frowned and tilted his head a little.

"It was your car." the Superintendent repeated slowly.

Wah shook his head and continued to look questioningly at the Superintendent. His car?

"I don't understand," Wah said. "And what did Inspector Choi want to know? Why does he go to you and not to me if it was my car?"

But no sooner had he uttered the sentence than his eyes snapped open.

"Ai Ling!" he exclaimed in horror.

The Superintendent looked down for a moment, but then he looked Wah in the eye.

"She's dead, Wah."

Wah looked at him with wide, expressionless eyes. This could not be. There had to be a mistake. Ai Ling could not be dead. She would probably already be in bed, asleep. She had probably cried herself to sleep in anger because he had not come to the restaurant for dinner as arranged. To make matters worse, he had only cancelled the meeting when Ai Ling was already sitting in the restaurant waiting for him.

"Choi was able to tell me, based on some witness statements, that Ai Ling entered the restaurant at around 8 p.m.. She received a phone call there, whereupon she paid for her drink and left. She had parked the car near the restaurant. She got in and a few seconds later the bomb exploded. - She was killed instantly."

The Superintendent fell silent.

Wah's throat felt tight. He stood up and tried to free himself from the tie. He felt as if the knot was tightening. Wah could hardly breathe. Finally he was able to pull the tie down. Hastily, he undid the top buttons of his shirt. His eyes wandered wildly and blankly around the office. Only with difficulty could he process the information he had just received.

"No!" Wah shouted suddenly, angrily firing the papers that were lying on his desk off the desk with his hands. Then he propped himself up on the edge of the desk with both hands. His head hung down.

There was silence in the office. Wah's shoulders shrugged. The Superintendent remained seated quietly and looked at Wah worriedly.

Wah had lost the love of his life. He no longer had a chance to apologise to Ai Ling. He no longer had a chance to make her a special breakfast and give her the necklace. He no longer had a chance to take her in his arms, kiss her and tell her he loved her. Instead, he had to tell their four-year-old daughter in the morning that her mama was no longer alive.

"Has... does anyone know... is there any lead yet?" asked Wah.

"No." replied Superintendent Lau. "Inspector Choi would like to know if you have any suspicions."

Wah shook his head.

"No. I... Not that I know of."

"Could the Yi Wong be behind this? Maybe as a warning to stop the investigation?" the Superintendent inquired.

Wah ran his hand over his face and then through his hair. He could no longer think clearly.

"I don't know."

16 June 2005, 6:30 am, London

Tung Ming Wah woke up in a cold sweat. That dream again. He took a few deep breaths and looked around. Yes, he was home. At home. A glance at the alarm clock told him it was six thirty. Wah exhaled loudly and swung himself out of bed. In half an hour he would have had to get up anyway. He went into the bathroom and took a hot shower. The water ran over his slim and well-toned body. Over the fine and lightly tanned skin of an Asian. Then he got dressed, went into the kitchen and brewed some tea.

"Mui."

He had knocked on her room door and entered. She was still asleep. He went to the window and pulled back the curtains. Then he sat down on the edge of the bed.

"Mui, get up."

With a low grumble, Mui turned around. She had trouble opening her eyes. Her long black hair hung tangled in her face. He brushed a strand behind her ear. Now he could see her face.

'She is becoming more like her mother,' he thought to himself.

"Good morning!" he said with a smile.

"Morning." Mui respondended sleepily.

"Hop out of bed. You have to go to school."

Mui curled up.

"I don't want to" she grumbled.

"Yes, you do."

"I don't feel good at all though."

17

Mui tried hard to sound as sickly as possible. Wah laughed, got up and pulled the covers away.

"Get out," he called to her with a laugh.

"I'm really not feeling well." growled Mui, trying to catch the blanket.

"I bet you'll feel better after the maths quiz." he teased her.

Mui tilted her head. How did he know that again?

"Off to the bathroom." he said in a light commanding tone.

All the begging and moaning did not help. She had to go to school. Mui stood up. She stretched a little and then shuffled listlessly to the bathroom.

Wah put the duvet back on the bed and opened the window. Fresh spicy air entered the room. Since her mother's death, a picture of Ai Ling had been on Mui's night table. A lump formed in his throat. How much he missed Ai Ling.

He went out and closed the door behind him.

Wah drove Mui to school like every morning. He opened her door and she got out.

"Bye." she called to him and walked towards the school.

He had to think of the dream again.

"Mui."

She turned to him and looked at him questioningly. Wah walked towards her.

"I love you. " he said softly with a smile.

"Yes, yes, it's all right. I love you too," she replied quickly.

She looked around. Hopefully the others hadn't noticed. She was embarrassed. Wah's smile became a broad grin. 'Girls,' he thought, amused. He got back into the car, waved to her again and drove off.

At that moment, Maryanne approached Mui.

"Hi."

"Hi." replied Mui.

Maryanne looked after the car.

"Your dad is *so* cool!" she gushed, sighing softly - just like they always did in the romance movies Maryanne watched every night.

Mui rolled her eyes. Many of her classmates - and some of their single mothers - fancied Mui's father. More or less obviously. Okay, he was good-looking. Despite his age and the grey streaks, he still looked quite young. his beard even gave him something dashing. He was slim and cut an excellent figure in any outfit, whether in a suit or jeans and jumper. And it was a lot of fun being him. Nevertheless, Mui thought that the others were exaggerating their crush on him.

"Did you prepare for the quiz?" asked Mui, changing the subject.

Maryanne sighed again, but this time it was a very different sigh.

"I've tried. But I just don't get it. I think I'm going to blow this one to smithereens. What about you?"

"As usual." said Mui indifferently.

Maryanne shook her head.

"I wish learning would come as easily to me as it

does to you!"

Both went into the school building.

Wah drove through the congested streets of London. He was not moving fast. At nine o'clock he had to be at the meeting of the Development and Analysis Unit, a department within the intelligence service the Metropolitan Police in London, to which he had belonged for a few years. He had come to this post through connections...

Wah was stunned. It was as if the ground had been pulled away from under him. As if his livelihood had been snatched away from him. It took him several minutes to regain his composure. The Superintendent had remained sitting quietly the whole time. Normally, he had to tell the wife that her husband had been killed during duty. This situation was new for him.

"Is it all right?" he asked.

Wah nodded briefly. He tried to smile, but with his lips pressed together it became a grimace. The Superintendent stood up. There was nothing more he could do. Wah had to deal with the grief. Superintendent Lau thought of little Mui. It would be hard growing up without a mother.

"You are on leave for a fortnight. I'll take care of the rest here with Nie Wen. - I am truly sorry, Wah," he added in a low tone.

Wah nodded. Then Superintendent Lau left the office.

Wah energetically ran his hands through his hair. How could he tell Mui? And he also had to inform Ai Ling's parents, with whom Mui was staying tonight. Again Wah looked at the picture beside the screen. He couldn't imagine what life would be like without Ai Ling. He closed his eyes, took a deep breath and stood up. There was no point in dragging it out any longer. He left his office.

Nie Wen was now sitting alone in the open-plan office. He was twelve years younger than Wah and had been assigned to him as a partner directly after police school. Over the past five years, they had become best friends. When Wah stepped out of the office shortly after the Superintendent, Nie Wen looked at him inquiringly.

Wah saw him, but only raised his hand briefly to show that he wanted his peace. He didn't want to speak. He mustered up all his strength pulling himself together. His chest ached and he could hardly breathe. Nie Wen nodded and turned back to the paper in his hand.

Finally Wah drove into the underground car park of the Metropolitan Police ("Met"), better known as Scotland Yard. 08:49. He would be on time.

16 June 2005, 12:45, China Town, London

The restaurant was noisy and the air was heavy with the spicy smell of the various Chinese dishes on the tables. It was lunch time. Some took advantage of the cheap lunch menu, others took their business partners out à la carte. An ornate partition wall made of dark wood separated an alcove from the large room. It protected from the guests' gaze, but one could easily see into the busy hall. In the alcove was a rectangular table that could seat four people comfortably.

Wah briefly looked around the restaurant. At a large round table in the back corner of the restaurant, he finally spotted Tang Kwong Liu, commonly known as Fat Liu, studying the menu. A large pot of tea was already on the table. Fat Liu was fat, greedy and loyal only to himself. He had been Wah's informant for over six years and for food he would probably even sell his mother, Wah surmised. However, he always gave reliable information and knew his way around London's China Town. He knew the old families, the new arrivals and also knew a lot about the relationships and disputes among the triads. Wah always wondered why the triads left Fat Liu alone. He must have had a very good life insurance that nothing had happened to him yet. For he was well known for his talkativeness. As Wah walked towards the table, he looked closely at the people sitting in the restaurant today. When he arrived at the table, Fat Liu barely looked up from the menu.

"Sit down, Tung. I hope you have the company credit card with you today, I have a mighty appetite."

Wah gave a brief smile and sat down. Just then, the waitress arrived in a dark blue qipao.

"What would you like to drink?" she turned to Wah.

"A Tsingtao, please."

As Fat Liu was still leafing through the menu, the waitress left the table again.

Wong Wei Yan sat alone at the table behind the partition and waited for his best friend, Robert Duncan. To pass the time, Yan observed the hustle and bustle in the restaurant. A slim Chinese man with slightly greying hair and a beard had just walked across the room of the restaurant. He was wearing a dark blue suit, a white shirt, a blue-striped tie and black leather shoes. The arrival went to a table in the opposite corner of Yan's alcove, where a fat Chinese man was already seated. As the arrival sat with his back to the wall, Yan could see his face clearly.

Somehow the man seemed familiar to him. But from where? Yan looked at him more closely. Study? No. Business? No. Or? Suddenly Yan's eyes snapped open. He looked as if he had seen a ghost. And that's exactly what he thought.

"That is not possible," Yan said quietly.

He was horrified. 'It can't be. He is dead! He must be dead!' His thoughts went round in circles. But there was no doubt: not ten metres away from him sat Tung Ming Wah.

Tung Ming Wah! The man who was responsible for his father's death. Yan took out his mobile phone and dialled a number.

When Robert Duncan arrived, he found his friend lost in thought. Something seemed to be preoccupying Yan. He had an absent look on his face. But when he noticed Robert, his expression changed immediately. He stood up and greeted his friend with a radiant smile. They shook hands.

"How are you, Yan?" asked Robert.

"I'm fine. And you?" Yan evaded.

He had known Robert since he was a student. Robert had helped him out of a situation once during that time and gradually gained more and more of Yan's trust. Robert knew Yan's business, so he could trust him. Still, he wasn't sure yet whether he should tell Robert about his discovery. - Maybe later.

"Nice to see you again. I see not much has changed since my last visit to London," Yan noted.

"True. Not much has changed in the last four months." Robert teased him.

"When are *you* coming to Hong Kong again?" countered Yan.

"Yan, don't tempt me." Robert rolled his eyes and began to smile. A few days of rest would do him good.

"You can spend the night at my place. After all, the flat has three bedrooms.... "

Robert waved it off with a laugh.

"Yan, you sound like you're getting brokerage fees for this. - I know your flat and I thank you for the generous offer. But when I come, I will go back to the hotel. Thank you."

"Hotel. Hotel. Hotel is impersonal. - Why don't you finally buy a flat in Hong Kong?"

"Firstly, it always depends on the hotel and secondly on what you want, Yan. I want to keep my independence. I check in, I check out. Whenever I feel like it. I don't have to make arrangements about what to do when I'm not there. Possession can also be a hindrance."

"And this from someone whose family owns a large country estate in England."

Robert laughed. "That's why I know."

"I'm serious, Robert. You might as well afford a flat at Highcliff. It's not even two and a half million pounds. You could easily afford that. Besides, you speak perfect Cantonese and Mandarin. You could even get a job in Hong Kong with no problem. In case you got bored."

"Yan, stop promising me heaven," Robert laughingly rebuffed. "You know exactly how much I love Hong Kong. To live there entirely would mean a dream come true. But what on earth would I need a 700 square metre flat?"

"You're joking! Your parents' house is more than ten times bigger!"

"This is exactly why I have an aversion to large flats."

Yan laughed. He knew that Robert's father would be struck dead if he had just heard his son's remark.

"Don't make such a fuss. I live in it alone too. Well, there's Ruby..."

"Oh, how is she?" inquired Robert with interest.

"Ruby? Good. She's still running the show and doesn't want anything taken away from her. But I think she probably won't be able to continue soon. I have already reserved a place for her in an exclusive home. She deserves it," Yan said about his old maid, who had already served as his father's maid when Yan was born.

"If I had a Ruby like that too, I probably wouldn't find it so hard."

"Imagine Robert, you could go bowling more often then." Yan tried to tease him. He could not understand his friend's passion for bowling. Especially since, strangely enough, he only ever pursued his passion in Hong Kong. But he did so with great fervour.

"Yan, stop it! I'll get a hotel room, as usual," Robert defended himself.

"So you're coming back to Hong Kong?!" exclaimed Yan joyfully.

While they ate, the two friends thought about all the things they wanted to do during Robert's visit to Hong Kong. But Yan kept looking past Robert into the dining room. Which did not escape Robert's attention at all.

"Yan, what's wrong?" asked Robert straightforwardly.

"What do you mean?"

"What's so interesting back there that you have to keep looking. Has the woman of your dreams entered? Then stand up and propose to her."

"No. It's more like a walking nightmare that I

discovered."

"The tax investigation?" Robert teased him.

Yan scowled at Robert.

"No. - My father's murderer."

"What?!" Robert's eyes snapped open and he turned around.

"Where?"

"Back there in the corner. At the table with the loud fat guy."

"This is the policeman?"

"Yes."

Robert sat down properly again and looked Yan in the eye. The latter held his gaze. After a few seconds of silence, Robert shook his head and leaned forward.

"But at that time there was a huge bounty on his head. The whole Hong Kong underworld was looking for him."

"I know. He suddenly disappeared off the face of the earth. After five years I was sure he had to be dead."

Robert laughed briefly, shook his head again.

"Unbelievable! - And then you see him just walk in here like that. What are you going to do now?" asked Robert.

"I don't know yet."

Yan looked through the partition, lost in thought. Didn't he already have enough problems of his own?

"So you're coming to Hong Kong for sure?" Yan suddenly inquired.

"Yes. That's what we've been talking about all along."

Robert was surprised. Did Yan still have something on his mind?

"Do you need me?"

"Could be." said Yan vaguely.

"Are you in trouble?"

"Could be. But I don't know for sure yet."

"Are you being blackmailed?"

Yan furrowed his eyebrows reproachfully.

"No! - I just have a suspicion that it's not quite what it seems."

"Business, then? Yan, I need more precise information about what's going on if I'm to help you," Robert urged Yan.

"If I knew exactly, I could regulate it myself. I have a suspicion that not everyone is abiding by the new structure. There's been the odd warning, which I'd only ever dismissed as a 'silly-boy prank'. But it seems to be rather carefully planned."

"Is it coming from the Yi Wong or the competition?"

"I am afraid that this is from within the Yi Wong."

"Who would dare to overthrow the Chairman?"

"The Chairman has changed direction and not everyone is happy about it." Yan pointed out. "It would be good if you could keep an eye on my surroundings from time to time."

"You can count on me."

"Thank you." Yan was relieved. At least one human being was on his side.

Today's conversation with Fat Liu today was not nearly as interesting as usual. Wah ate slowly and listened to the loudly smacking Fat Liu, who was once again talking about the good old days in China Town.

"Liu, you said you had some news for me. I have already noticed that China Town is no longer the same as it was twenty years ago. I myself have seen many restaurants and shops close down in the last seven years. But I'm here because you said you had some interesting news for me."

Wah was annoyed. He had been sitting here for two hours and had not heard any news. The bill would be high again and he didn't want to hand the Superintendent the bill without at least being able to say that it had been worth it.

In the meantime, the restaurant had emptied out.

Two men stepped out of the opposite alcove. Wah estimated their age to be in their late twenties. One was a tall, slim Chinese man with distinctive facial features. He was dressed in a black turtleneck jumper, black trousers and black shoes. The other man was a European, tall, normal build with short dark brown hair. He was wearing jeans, a black polo shirt and a greenish corduroy blazer.

Both looked briefly over at Wah, even looked him straight in the eye, and then left the restaurant. Wah turned back to Fat Liu.

"You are far too impatient. - And you don't eat

enough, Tung," the Fat Liu countered.

But he saw Wah's expression and lowered his voice a little. "A Dragon Head from Hong Kong is here."

"Here? In the restaurant?"

"No. In London."

"What is he doing here?"

"Open a branch? Maybe?"

"Maybe?"

"After all, he has to come to an agreement with the local triads first."

"Name?"

"I don't know yet."

"How many members?"

"About seven thousand. Relatively small."

"It's not that small."

"Hmm."

"Which district in Hong Kong?"

"Hong Kong Island."

"What else?"

"Nothing."

"What?"

"Nothing. I haven't heard anything more."

"And for this you waste my time?"

"Hey, slow down. This information is new. And you're the first person I've told. Just found out last night."

"Where did you get the information?"

Fat Liu smiled appraisingly at Wah. Wah grinned.

"It was worth a try."

Fat Liu held his napkin in front of his mouth and laughed, grunting to himself.

An hour later, Wah stepped out of the restaurant. He turned left and walked to the nearest underground station. Due to the meeting in the morning and the long lunch with Fat Liu, he had not yet been able to do any real work. And the files on his desk were piling up. But such meetings were also an important part of his work. Or rather, an interesting addition to his tasks, as he called it.

6 July 1998, 18:00, Hong Kong Island

Yan entered his father's study. Since his arrival in Hong Kong, he had hardly had a minute all by himself. He had had some commitments and appointments to attend to. Now he closed the door behind him. Peace at last! Slowly he walked towards the large desk. Everything was still as his father had left it. Yan had the feeling that his father would have to enter the room and sit down at his desk any time. But he did not come. He could not come. He was dead.

Now Yan sat in the big comfortable leather chair behind the desk. He leaned back. The Yi Wong counted a few thousand members. Not to be compared with the 14K or Sun Yee On. In some triads, the Chairman was elected every few years. In the Yi Wong, this position was transferred from father to son. Now Yan was the Dragon Head.

And Yan hated this tradition. He hated it just as much as he detested and rejected his father's business. But he could not escape it. Yan had grown up in the syndicate, his father had trained him from an early age for the role of the future Chairman of the Yi Wong. But how could the only son escape his harsh father, who was used to power? It was only when Yan had the opportunity to study in London that he escaped his father.

Life had been different in London. Very different. Far away from his father and the syndicate. In London, Yan had lived the life he had always wanted. He studied, he had English friends. He had Alison. A normal life. With Alison. - At the thought of her, a pained smile stole onto his face. Alison. How much he missed her. And he wondered if this pain would ever let him go.

A servant of his father entered the room and brought Yan back to the present. The servant placed the glass of wine that Yan had ordered on the desk and left the room again.

Yan realised again why he was here. As much as he detested all the circumstances that came with it, the sudden, violent death of his father had shaken him. He still could not believe it.

How often had his father told him that he had the responsibility over a large family. How often had his father told him never to put himself in danger. Never take a risk. There were others for that. And yet his father had done just that. He himself had taken part in this transaction. For the sake of good old times and the friendship that bound him to the supplier. He had insisted on it. Although there was already a rumour that someone from the Narcotics Bureau of the Hong Kong Police Force was on his trail. That could not deter him.

'Yan,' Wong Zhao Wen had assured his son on the phone, 'don't worry about the policeman. He won't be a nuisance much longer.'

But things turned out differently. No sooner had the transaction been completed than armed police units suddenly entered the building. This was despite the fact that Wong Zhao Wen had brought the transaction forward at short notice and changed the place of delivery. Wong Zhao Wen had taken the risk. And he had lost. Yan closed his eyes. The whole thing made no sense. Why had his father insisted on participating in the transaction? And what had his father meant on the phone? What had made him so sure that nothing would go wrong? After all, not everyone could be bought.

Yan rose. He went to the safe, which was hidden behind a large framed calligraphy. The combination of numbers was the anniversary of Yan's mother's death. The door opened. He immediately noticed a large envelope. He took it out and went back to the desk. In the envelope he found a note from his father, as well as some photographs. The photographs showed the same man over and over again. Yan did not know him. However, he could tell from the note that this was the policeman who was targeting the syndicate. Nothing else was noted. Yan reached for the phone.

Kwong Wai Ming entered the room. He was not very tall, slim and gave the impression of an uptight accountant. His short grey hair stood out from his head and he wore round glasses. A bit too big for his face. But he had been Wong Zhao Wen's best friend and close confidant. His death grieved him at least as much as Yan.

'Maybe even more,' Yan said. Yan had not had a good relationship with his father before. But since he had taken Alison away from him, Yan had reduced contact to the bare minimum.

Nevertheless, Yan sought revenge for his father's death. He hoped that Kwong Wai Ming could shed light on the matter. Yan stood up and greeted the elderly gentleman respectfully.

When Kwong Wai Ming left the room again three hours later, Yan had made a decision: This policeman had to be held accountable.

He would see to that!

24 June 2005, 9:45 am, London

"What is it, Superintendent?" asked Wah as he entered the office and closed the door behind him.

On Superintendent Alcott's desk was a large envelope and some large format prints of photographs.

"Sit down, Wah. This has just been delivered by a courier."

With these words, he handed Wah the prints. Mui was depicted in all the pictures. Wah pressed his lips together.

"The Flying Squad is already on its way to your daughter's school to prevent a possible kidnapping," the Superintendent explained.

Wah exhaled loudly and buried his face in his hands. His eyes burned, his throat ached and his chest tightened.

'Not Mui!' he thought in horror. 'Not Mui too!'

His thoughts began to race.

When Superintendent Alcott spoke again, Wah raised his head to look the Superintendent in the eye. He had himself under control again.

"Could it be that you have stepped on someone's toes?"

"Not that I know of."

"Does it have anything to do with Fat Liu, perhaps?"

"What would that have to do with Fat Liu?"

"He was found dead in the boot of his car this

morning. He had been butchered. The coroners are examining him now."

Wah leaned back in the chair. He stared into a corner of the office. Strange. For years the triads had left him alone, and now suddenly he was murdered? Depending on what Fat Liu had deposited as insurance, things could get extremely restless in China Town or the whole of England. Even triad wars would not be out of the question. But who would murder him? And why? He had passed on more explosive information before and not a hair was turned on his head. Was there a connection between the murder and Mui's pictures? What the hell had Mui got to do with it? - The Superintendent snapped him out of his thoughts.

"You had met with him last week, hadn't you?"

"Yes."

"What was it about?"

"It was about a Dragon Head from Hong Kong who seems to want to settle here. The syndicate is said to be based mainly in Hong Kong Island. About seven thousand members."

"What else?"

"I haven't been able to find out anything else so far."

"And you didn't notice anyone in the restaurant?"

"The restaurant was full."

"Jeez, you're a policeman! I can't accept that excuse."

Wah went over the three hours with Fat Liu again in his mind.

"There were these two men. They had been sitting behind the carved partition that separates the niche from the big room."

"Businessmen?"

"Hardly."

"What kind of men were they?"

"A tall, slim Chinese man and a European."

"Do you know them?"

Wah looked at Superintendent Alcott with raised eyebrows. He did not like having to answer unnecessary questions. After all, if he had known the men, he would have said so already.

"Can you describe the men?"

"Yes."

"Did you notice anyone else?"

"No."

"Well. - Have Marty check who reserved the alcove that day. Then go to Johnson and have sketches made. Maybe that's a lead."

"What about Mui?"

"Mui is being brought here. As soon as she arrives, we'll let you know."

"And then?"

"We will take you and your daughter to a secured flat. You should still give us a list of what you need from your house in Ealing. Until we know who is behind this, you should not enter the house again."

Wah got up and left the room. He immediately went to Johnson on the fifth floor.

"Hello Wah!" Johnson called out to him.

"Hi Peter."

"The grey fox has already told me. We can start right away." Peter grinned.

Peter Johnson was a man in his forties, but he looked like he was still living in the eighties. He still wore his big glasses and those colourful Hawaiian shirts, carrot jeans and white socks. But as crazy as he looked, he was an excellent policeman. He used to work undercover. But his cover was blown one day and he was more dead than alive when he was found. Since then he was in a wheelchair and could only move his right arm. He was a fighter. Did not give up. And had specialised in creating phantom images with his talent for drawing. Wah and all the other colleagues admired him.

Wah began the descriptions and after forty-five minutes Johnson had produced accurate sketches of the two men.

"Please give me a copy of the files when you're done?"

"Why?"

Wah looked him in the eye and smiled weakly.

"Don't trust us, do you?" teased Johnson.

"It has nothing to do with that."

Johnson laughed.

No sooner had Wah returned to his desk than Superintendent Alcott approached him. The

Superintendent looked at Wah with concern.

"Wah. - Please come with me to my office." the Superintendent said quietly.

Just the look on Superintendent Alcott's face confirmed Wah's concern that the police had arrived too late at Mui's school. Wah closed his eyes and tried to take a deep breath. When he opened his eyes again, he looked at the framed picture next to his monitor....

'No one can run from their past,' he thought and slowly rose to follow the Superintendent into his office.

25 June 2005, 14:27, London, Ealing

The team of investigators had set up all necessary equipments and measurements in Wah's house. The wiretap specialists had set up their computers on the dining table. There was no news from the kidnappers yet.

Inspector Buchanan, who was leading the investigation into the abduction of Ai Mui, was sitting in the living room with his team and Wah. On the living room table were the sketches and a few other documents.

Inspector Buchanan began the meeting.

"The European has been identified as Robert Duncan. Comes from a wealthy family. Studied in London but has no professional activities. Parents are divorced. Duncan had a half-sister named Alison who died in a car accident a few years ago. There are no charges against him. - This morning we received a response from Interpol. Hong Kong Police Force has identified the Chinese man as Wong Wei Yan. He is the Dragon Head of a syndicate called..."

"Yi Wong." Wah finished the sentence.

"Right."

Inspector Buchanan looked at Wah with interest.

"What do you know about them? Did you have any dealings with them in Hong Kong?"

Wah nodded.

"I had investigated the Yi Wong in Hong Kong. The syndicate runs its business mainly on Hong Kong Island. It had taken months to get enough evidence and information to finally crack down and hopefully annihilate the syndicate. When the time finally came and we intervened in a narcotics transfer, there was an exchange of gunfire. The Dragon Head of the Yi Wong, who had taken part in the transaction himself, was shot dead in the process. We had dealt a bitter blow to the syndicate, but it had by no means been crushed. His son, Wong Wei Yan, then became the Dragon Head of the syndicate. He had put a large bounty on my head. Almost the entire Hong Kong underworld was looking for me.

"A solution could be found at a higher level and so I resigned from the Hong Kong Police Force in the strictest secrecy and started working for the Met. Only my former partner, Chow Nie Wen, who is also my best friend, knew about it. To everyone else, I had simply disappeared."

"Anything else I should know?" asked Buchanan.

"On the same day that we took action against the Yi Wong, my wife was killed by a car bomb. Probably a warning from the Yi Wong not to interfere in their affairs. But it could never be proved."

Inspector Buchanan and his people's eyes widened. When Wah reported this, one would have thought that none of this would affect him personally, so calmly did he sit there. Inspector Buchanan shook his head.

'Asians. Just don't lose your temper in front of others. That would be tantamount to losing face. Even when it comes to one's own family,' the inspector thought respectfully. He had had a lot of dealings with Asians. He knew their culture and their codes of behaviour. He knew what *guanxi* meant and how much it could hinder investigations. One fought against a wall of silence that could only be broken through little by little. One had to know the rules in order to discover small niches and use them for investigations. This knowledge had always served him well in investigations. Which is why he was also responsible for leading this investigation.

But mostly the cases were within one municipality. This situation was different. As Inspector Buchanan had already learned, Inspector Tung had no contact with the Chinese in the London commune. And from what he had just heard, he knew why. Here he would probably not come into contact with the follow-up problems of *Guanxi.* On the other hand, this now also made the investigation a little more difficult.

"So could it be that you have been recognised?"

"Maybe."

"Had you seen Wong Wei Yan before?"

"No. He was in England at the time. - Besides, I would have recognised him in the restaurant."

The inspector raised his eyebrows.

"Do you know what he was doing here?"

"When?"

"Back then."

"Studied."

"Can you tell me more?"

"No. I was too focused on his father," Wah answered briefly.

The inspector made notes. This is where he would investigate. He knew from the records that Robert Duncan had booked the table at the restaurant. It was just not known exactly where the two men had met. But now the pieces of the puzzle were slowly falling into place and a picture was beginning to emerge.

Then Robert Duncan probably knew Wong Wei Yan from his studies. However, since Robert Duncan was two years younger than Wong Wei Yan, they could hardly have taken the same courses. But something had connected the two men. They would find that out as well.

"Good, then we'll check whether Wong studied at the same university as Duncan. Maybe we'll find some clues there. In the meantime, the search continues here."

"It's like looking for a needle in a haystack, isn't it?" Wah remarked.

"We have no other choice, Mr. Tung, as long as the kidnappers do not come forward, we will just have to look for the needle."

Wah rubbed his chin. He felt helpless.

29 June 1998, 16:43, Hong Kong Island

Johnny Lee rose from the sofa. Clad only in a vest and shorts, he shuffled to the flat door in his flip-flops. He looked through the peephole in the flat door. A delivery boy was standing in front of the door. Full of joy for his dinner, Johnny Lee opened the wooden door and pulled the metal grille aside.

At that moment, Wah jumped down from the top of the stairs and pushed the delivery boy aside, who immediately ran away in fear. Wah threw himself against the door, which Johnny Lee quickly tried to close. Johnny Lee staggered backwards. Wah forced his way into the small flat, slammed the door and pounced on Johnny Lee.

"Hello, Johnny!"

"My God, Wah! You scared me to death!"

Johnny Lee tried to free himself.

"Yes, there was no mistaking the joy of seeing me."

Wah pushed Johnny Lee further into the living room.

"What are you doing here? Do you want me to be killed?"

Johnny Lee hoped that he could still get off lightly by pretending to be ignorant. But that only made Wah angrier.

"Why weren't you at the meeting place last night?"

Wah had Johnny Lee pressed against a wall. His arm pressed firmly against Johnny Lee's throat.

"I was busy. I was given some special assignments to do."

"Did those special assignments include sending some thugs after me?"

Wah let go of Johnny Lee. Just as he was about to relax, Wah hit him in the face with his fist without warning. Blood shot out of his nose. Johnny Lee cried out in pain and covered his broken nose with both hands. Blood ran down between his fingers.

"You son of a bitch broke my nose!" Johnny Lee screamed at him hysterically.

"If I don't get some useful information from you, I'll break you a lot more." Wah ordered him and raised his clenched fist again.

"You're crazy!"

Wah went on to take a further swing.

"Don't!"

"Did you send the goons after me?"

"No."

"You sure?"

"Yeah, damn. Maybe someone noticed I was passing on some information."

"Bullshit! Then you'd be lying on the floor in six pieces and you wouldn't be coming at me with such stupid answers." Wah remarked dryly.

Johnny Lee looked at him in horror.

"So what about the information?" echoed Wah.

"I haven't been able to find out anything yet."

Wah's fist shot out at Johnny Lee's nose again.

"You son of a bitch!" roared Johnny Lee in pain.

"What about the information?"

"I haven't got it yet! Shit! - Why don't you ask your partner?"

"Which one?" asked Wah in surprise.

"Well, your partner. Nie Wen."

"What has Nie Wen got to do with it?"

"You don't know? Hey, that guy is a son of Wong Zhao Wen!" said Johnny Lee gleefully. But the reaction he had hoped for failed to materialise.

"Tell me something I don't already know."

Wah took a step back. He had known Johnny Lee for a long time. And he knew him well enough to know that Johnny Lee spoke the truth. For his loyalty was as low as his pain threshold. Wah pulled himself together again. He was here because he wanted information about the Yi Wong's next drug transfer.

Based on Wah's statement and calm demeanour, Johnny Lee was the surprised one. Tung had known about this?

"Get me the information and don't you dare try to trick me."

"How am I supposed to get the information?"

"That's your problem. I want the information. See you in the morning."

"Do you think old Wong will announce the handover date in the paper?"

Wah grinned and pinched one of Johnny Lee's meaty cheeks. He turned the cheek a little. Johnny Lee, in even more pain from his twice-broken nose, began to whimper.

"See you - tomorrow morning!"

With that, he let go of Johnny Lee and left the flat.

Now he had to take care of Nie Wen. The tide had turned. Because now he had to have his best friend and partner shadowed. He simply had to have clarity as to whether or not he could continue to trust Nie Wen. This blood relationship with Wong Zhao Wen could not be allowed to ruin the investigation.

26 June 2005, 12:53, London, Ealing

"Have you been watching the news? It's been a hot time in China Town. The cops are making raid after raid. One arrest after another. Man, I don't want to have to write these reports right now." Williams shouted excitedly as he entered Wah's house.

Inspector Buchanan gave him a reproving look. They all knew the news. But they were not here to follow the work of their colleagues.

"Okay, Steve, you can go home. I'll take over." Williams now said much more quietly and also somewhat disappointedly to his colleague who had been on shift since the early hours of the morning.

How Williams would have liked to talk about the events in China Town, which also spread to other towns in England, and speculate about the background. But the inspector's look had reminded him again that the daughter of a colleague had been kidnapped.

Two days had passed since Ai Mui's abduction. And still no news from the kidnappers. Nerves were on edge. Inspector Buchanan sat in the living room of Wah's house in Ealing. He watched Wah standing at the window staring out. Wah knew the police procedure for kidnapping. That made Inspector Buchanan's job easier. However, Wah had a mind of his own and still kept in close contact with his best friend, Chow Nie Wen, in Hong Kong. And *that was* a thorn in the side of Inspector Buchanan and the team. Actually, Wah should know that outside contact was forbidden until the case was solved. After all, they never knew who was behind the kidnapping, and this prevented information from being passed on to the wrong people. But on this one point, regarding Nie Wen, Wah was intransigent and stubborn.

Wah had known for about seven years that Nie Wen was the illegitimate son of Wong Zhao Wen. He was, therefore, also the half-brother of the current Yi Wong Chairman, Wong Wie Yan. But Nie Wen did not seem to know this. Nor had he had any contact with the Yi Wong.

Since Wah had found out about it seven years ago, he had had him shadowed and also put to the test a few times. Nie Wen had definitely had no contact with Yi Wong or Wong Zhao Wen.

Suddenly the phone rang. At last! Wah walked up to the phone. After getting the okay from the wiretap specialist, he picked up the receiver.

"Hello?"

"Hello, may I speak to Nelly please?"

"You've got the wrong number."

"Oh. Sorry."

It clicked.

Wah put the receiver down noisily. The wiretap specialist was about to take off his headphones again when the phone rang again. Wah waited for the policeman's signal and picked up again.

"Hello?"

"Who am I talking to?"

Wah was surprised and looked at the Inspector.

"Tung Ming Wah."

The inspector's eyes snapped open and he looked at the wiretap specialist. The latter eagerly tried to trace the call as quickly as possible. But he was led from one country to another. The kidnappers were careful.

"I'll call you again in half an hour. Then I want to hear from you when you will arrive in Hong Kong and in which hotel you will stay!"

"All right."

The conversation was interrupted. Wah took a deep breath and slowly hung up the phone.

"What was that about?" asked Inspector Buchanan.

Wah sat down on the armrest of the sofa.

"The kidnappers will call again in half an hour. Then they want to know when I will arrive in Hong Kong and in which hotel I will stay."

"Hong Kong?!" the inspector exclaimed in surprise.

Wah ran a hand through his hair and stood up. He went to the window and looked out again. Inspector Buchanan went to the wiretap specialist. But he just shook his head, stared intently at the screen and tapped nervously on the keyboard. "Maybe a tap-proof satellite connection. I don't know for sure. They had a lot of stray calls upstream. The call was too short."

Wah looked at the clock, went to the phone again and picked up the receiver. He dialled a long number and waited until someone answered.

"Hello!" was the gruff reply.

Wah knew it was the middle of the night in Hong Kong. Nie Wen was probably already asleep.

"Hello Nie Wen, this is Wah. Can you recommend a hotel in Hong Kong?"

Short pause.

"Hong Kong?" asked Nie Wen in surprise.

All at once he was wide awake.

"The kidnappers have contacted me. In half an hour I have to tell them when I will arrive in Hong Kong and where I will stay," Wah replied.

"Then maybe Mui is already here..." said Nie Wen lost in thought, but then he recollected himself. "Why don't you go to the Novotel Century Harbourview?"

Wah drew his eyebrows together. 'Why did it come so quickly?' Since there are always several hotels in a city, locals usually had to think first about which hotel they would recommend. After all, as a local, you didn't have to have hotels in mind.

"I don't know that one," Wah replied.

"Hmm, you must have been gone by the time it opened." Nie Wen wondered aloud.

"And how do you know it?" asked Wah, slightly irritated.

"I live in the house across the street."

Wah had to grin.

"And where is that exactly?"

"Hong Kong Island, Western District, 508 Queens Road West. Listen, I'll book you a room there."

"No, the police can do that. They are busy with the flights anyway."

"Okay."

"Thank you."

"Don't mention it. Let me know when you get here."

Wah hung up. The inspector walked towards him.

"Mr. Tung, we are in the process of getting you on one of the British Airways flights to Hong Kong tomorrow. The first Cathay Pacific flight is already fully booked."

"Good. My friend recommended the Novotel Century Harbourview."

"We have already booked you a room."

"Then please rebook it."

The inspector raised his eyebrows.

"Try it, Williams." he reluctantly passed on the order.

"Inspector," Williams objected, "the shopping festival starts soon in Hong Kong. Rooms should be scarce..."

"How do you know?"

"I found out when I booked the room."

"Try it anyway."

Grumbling, the employee turned to his computer and got back to work. Time was running out.

After some back and forth, they finally got confirmation that Wah could indeed fly to Hong Kong the next day on British Airways flight BA0025. And a room was found for Wah at the Novotel Century Harbourview.

Now they had to wait for the second call. Eight minutes to go. The hand of the grandfather clock seemed to not move any further. Every second felt like an eternity to them.

Finally the phone rang again.

Robert had spent quite a while waiting in the taxi until finally Yan's limousine turned into Stubbs Road. He instructed the taxi driver to follow the limousine at some distance. When Yan's limousine finally stopped in the Western District and Yan got out, Robert also had the taxi driver stop. He saw Yan enter a house entrance and disappear inside. Robert got out and looked around. Directly behind him he spotted the Shek Tong Tsui Municipal Services Building. Since he knew that there was also a restaurant in these Municipal Centres, which were spread all over the respective districts, he went inside.

He took the lift to the second floor, where the restaurant was located. Robert entered and took a seat at a round table near the window. He had a clear view of the entrance through which Yan had entered the building. Robert ordered tea and two dishes of chicken. The food was very cheap and, as he could see shortly afterwards, excellently prepared. If the menu were not written exclusively in Cantonese characters, this would be an excellent insider tip for low-budget travellers. But he was not here to write an article for the 'Lonely Planet'.

So he ate the food in peace and continued to keep an eye on the entrance to the house. He knew that Yan had been getting involved in dangerous meetings lately. For lately he had been receiving more and more threatening letters and his ventures to legalise the Yi Wong had been sabotaged again and again.

Now Yan was on the lookout for the enemy within the Yi Wong. But to do so, he had to meet with informants and sometimes also with other Dragon Heads. Which was by no means without danger.

Nie Wen had just left the house and crossed the street when he suddenly saw Yan enter a house. This area was unusual for Yan. What was he doing here? Nie Wen went to the entrance where Yan had disappeared and memorised the house number. He wanted to know that more precisely.

To be able to observe the house better and inconspicuously, he decided to go to the restaurant in the Municipal Centre, which was opposite the house. He ate there from time to time, so it wouldn't be noticeable if he stopped by now.

When he got out of the lift and entered the restaurant, he was already greeted. Since he usually ate the same thing, he only confirmed the waiter's assumption and sat down at a free table by the window.

A foreigner was sitting at another table. Nie Wen was surprised. Foreigners were hardly ever here. Besides, he was dressed too well for the restaurant. When the waiter brought the foreigner his food, he spoke to the waiter in pure Cantonese. Besides, the foreigner looked familiar to him. Nie Wen ate in silence, kept looking at the entrance to the house and watching the foreigner. One thing was clear, they were both looking at the same house entrance. So the foreigner had to be interested in Yan. But in what way? He seemed to be English. And since things had become very restless in London's China Town at the moment, it could well be that it was a hired sniper scouting out his target. Nie Wen looked at the man closely so that he would definitely recognise him.

Mary entered Inspector Cheung's office.

"The papers from the Liaison Bureau have just arrived," she said, placing the papers on the desk.

Inspector Cheung picked up the folder and distributed the contents to his staff after a brief viewing.

"Are the sketches included?"

"Yes. - Here. The Met has already had these images analysed by us. The Chinese man in question is Wong Wei Yan. He has been the Dragon Head of the Yi Wong since his father was shot dead in a police operation seven years ago."

"The Met thinks he's behind the kidnapping?"

"Wouldn't be far-fetched. Wong Wei Yan had blamed Tung for his father's death and put a bounty on his head. Tung went into hiding. Years later, Yan discovers him by chance in London and also finds out that Tung has a daughter. What better way to take revenge on him or force him to come back than to kidnap his daughter?"

"Has Tung been told this assumption yet?"

"When he was told the name of the Chinese man, he considered that possibility himself."

"That means we would only have to shadow a few of the Yi Wong people and get to the little girl?" asked Keung.

"I doubt they will make it that easy for us. - When does Tung's plane land?"

"The plane is scheduled to land shortly after 1 p.m.."

Inspector Cheung looked at his watch.

"Then we still have a little time before we have to go. - Does he know he's being picked up?"

"Yes. He'll be intercepted as soon as he enters the country and taken to the car. - You know him from before, don't you?"

The inspector nodded.

"Yes. We went to the police academy together. He later joined the Narcotics Bureau. From time to time we had exchanged information."

"What's he like?"

"Stubborn. Had his teeth into Wong Zhao Wen. He was almost obsessed. But he was also a professional. Knew how far he could go. He demanded one hundred percent commitment. But when there were problems, he had always stood by his people and remained fair."

"Does anyone know what happened to Chow Nie Wen?"

"We have our eye on him," Ming replied.

"Does Tung continue to keep in touch with him?"

"Yes. Unfortunately. Tung had called him again from the airport shortly before his departure. - He won't let us talk to him."

"See that Chow doesn't get in our way."

"What if we all work together?" asked Mary. "After

all, Chow was a policeman too."

"But he isn't any more. Besides, he'd be too biased anyway. He is Mui's godfather."

"But the kidnappers wouldn't count on him. He could be our trump card."

The men merely gave Mary a punishing sideways glance and turned back to the documents and protocols that the Metropolitan Police Services, London, had sent them via the Liaison Bureau. They had to leave in half an hour.

28 June 2005, 20:45, Hong Kong Island

Wah got out of the lift. He was tired. The long flight and the talks with the police had left their mark. Wah had had trouble convincing his companions that he was really just visiting a friend. They were as unenthusiastic here as the police in London about his keeping close contact with Nie Wen. They had let him go, but there were two policemen waiting for him outside the building. He pressed the bell button and after a short while the wooden door was opened.

Nie Wen almost no longer recognised his friend. Wah had lost a lot of weight, his hair had turned completely grey in the last few days and there were dark shadows around his eyes. No longer comparable to the picture Wah had sent to Nie Wen last month by e-mail together with Mui.

"You look like shit." greeted Nie Wen to his friend.

"Thank you. I'm glad to see you too," Wah countered.

Nie Wen now also opened the sliding metal door.

"Just straight ahead. You can't miss the living room. In five steps you'll be inside." laughed Nie Wen.

He closed both doors and followed Wah into the room.

It did Wah good to see Nie Wen again after all this time. The last time he had seen him, Nie Wen wore his black hair quite short. Now he had an almost shoulder-length mane, which he had dyed dark red. In his jeans and white T-shirt, Nie Wen looked even taller and thinner than he had a few years ago.

"How long have you lived here?" asked Wah,

looking around the small flat.

"Four years. - Sit down."

"Oh yes, I had forgotten. Sorry."

"No problem."

Wah sat down on the sofa.

"Well, for a bachelor, this is really fussy. Do you have a girlfriend?"

"Are you crazy? For her to make a mess here?" Nie Wen exclaimed in horror. "Besides, I can barely get myself through life. I'm not going to saddle myself with someone else."

"How are you?" asked Nie Wen a moment later.

"Guess... - Do you have any beer?"

Nie Wen went into the small kitchen and came back with two cans. He sat down cross-legged on the carpet in front of the sofa and looked at Wah calmly. They both drank their beer.

"I failed, Nie Wen." said Wah suddenly.

"In what way?"

"I should have recognised Wong Wei Yan in that restaurant in London. I should have recognised him! But I didn't. And because I didn't, Mui was kidnapped!"

Wah stood up hastily.

"I failed as a father and as a policeman!"

He ran his fingers wildly through his short hair. It was outside. What he had been carrying around with him for the last few days, he had now said out loud. Nie Wen was the only person Wah could be so open with.

Nie Wen remained sitting quietly. After a short while he said thoughtfully.

"You are only human, Wah! - Wong Wei Yan is no longer the boy he was a few years ago. You are an excellent policeman and I have never seen such a loving father interacting with his daughter. After Ai Ling's death, you had to be her father and mother. And I think you've managed that admirably."

Nie Wen stood up and walked towards Wah.

"Wah! Look at me!"

Wah turned away from the window and looked Nie Wen in the face.

"You haven*'t* failed. Don't beat yourself up. The kidnappers are already trying to do that. If you want to help Mui, you have to put those thoughts aside."

Wah looked at Nie Wen for a while and thought about the words. Nie Wen was right. He had to be strong for Mui too. It had done him good to let his guilty conscience run free. But now he had to pull himself together again. For Mui!

"How's the detective agency going?" asked Wah to change the subject. He sat down again.

"It's all right. I have enough orders to survive."

"Have you been able to find out anything yet?"

"No. - At least not much. There's a lead I'm following."

"What is it?"

"It's not concrete enough yet. Trust me. As soon as I am sure, I will send you and the police information."

Wah did not like the answer. But he had to accept

it. He had worked with Nie Wen at the Hong Kong Police Force for too long. Nie Wen had always done his research properly before approaching Wah with information.

Nie Wen pulled Wah out of his thoughts.

"It's not so easy anymore. A few informants have gone underground. Since there have been these riots between the syndicates in London, there have been more public confrontations here as well."

"Fat Liu had really built up a very good life insurance policy. No wonder he had been left alone all these years."

"One of them wouldn't leave him alone, though."

"Whoever did this, however, must now also reckon with proper trouble."

"Do you think he was too close to something after all?"

"I don't know. But the triads knew they were cutting their own flesh. The last time we had met, he had told me about the plans of a syndicate that probably wanted to set up in England. He couldn't give me names or details at the time. From what I know now, it all fits very well with the Yi Wong."

"Only it can't be proven yet. Whether it was intentional?"

"To deliberately cause the current chaos in London to erupt? So that they could grab each other's businesses while they're being arrested by the police or fighting each other?"

Wah looked doubtfully at Nie Wen.

"Could be, couldn't it?"

"The syndicates in England still have their Heads in Hong Kong. So that would cause powerful trouble here too."

"At least it has already become quite restless."

"That would put powerful pressure on Wong Wei Yan."

"Maybe he's playing a double game?"

"The risk would be too great. No sensible person would ever dare to do that."

"What if he does?"

Wah looked at Nie Wen. That would also throw Hong Kong into chaos. It could even have a negative impact on the world economy.

"Triad war?"

"Or just a diversionary tactic with an economic side effect..."

Wah stared at the ground in front of him. If it was planned, then he had little chance of getting Mui back alive. But would the Yi Wong go that far? Or maybe they weren't after all? Was there someone else behind the Yi Wong? Why would a relatively small syndicate mess with the Sun Yee On or the 14K? That would be crazy. It would be tantamount to suicide.

"Do you remember the chase through Wan Chai?" asked Nie Wen abruptly.

Wah nodded.

"Was a huge mess when we finally stopped those guys."

"The car was totalled after that," Wah said, rolling his eyes upwards.

Nie Wen grinned.

"Gee, what a trouble we were in afterwards."

"Should have asked the Chief Inspector for permission before we borrowed his car." Wah remarked dryly and took a last sip from the can.

A smile spread across Wah's face. Then he looked at Nie Wen, who gave him a broad grin.

"It was a great time already."

"I bet the insurance company was happy as a lark when the Hong Kong Police Force got rid of us."

After a while, Nie Wen got up and went to a dresser. He picked up a mobile phone and handed it to Wah.

"Here is a mobile phone with a prepaid card. My number is already stored. Call as soon as there's any news."

"Will do."

Wah looked out of the living room window. The Novotel Century Harbourview was almost parallel to Nie Wah's building.

"I have room 2206, right on the corner. I'll leave the curtains open."

Wah stood up.

"We'll talk again tomorrow."

"Yeah. Take care."

Nie Wen accompanied him to the door and waited until the lift doors closed behind Wah.

29 June 2005, 8:07 a.m., Hong Kong Island

Wah opened the door and reached for the newspaper, which was in a clear plastic bag attached to the doorknob. He rubbed his spiky chin and shuffled back to the bed. He was tired. It had taken him a while to fall asleep. His head was throbbing and he felt like it was still the middle of the night. Darn jet lag. He sat down on the bed and opened the newspaper. An envelope fell out. He picked it up and was about to throw it carelessly onto the window sill cushion when he realised it wasn't an advertisement. He swallowed, stared at the envelope and put it on the desk. He picked up the phone and dialled a number. Less than five minutes later, there was a knock at the door of the room. Wah stood up and looked through the peephole. Officer Cheng was standing outside. He opened the door.

"Good morning, sir!"

"Good morning. The envelope is on the desk. It was hidden in the newspaper."

"You've already opened it?!" Officer Cheng exclaimed in surprise when he saw the open letter lying on the desk.

Wah looked at him sullenly.

"Of course! My daughter has been kidnapped!"

A little calmer, Wah added, "I did pick it up by hand and put it on the desk, but I only opened it with tweezers. Please don't forget that I am also a policeman, officer."

Officer Cheng put on gloves and put the newspaper was in, the newspaper and the letter in separate evidence bags, labelled them and left the room.

"I'll take it to headquarters right away."

"I'll be right there, too."

"Officer Wong will wait for you and take you to the headquarters, sir."

"Thank you."

"Goodbye."

"Goodbye."

Wah closed the door. He took the mobile phone Nie Wen had given him and dialled.

"Hello!"

"Did you see it all?"

"Yes. Is the note being examined yet?"

"Yes. Just picked up."

"Okay, get ready. I'll be there."

"You may be shadowed."

"Very likely," laughed Nie Wen.

He knew the police procedure. And he knew that Wah's contact with him was a thorn in the police's side.

"Okay."

Wah went into the bathroom and took a hot shower.

One hour later Wah arrived at the Crime Wing Regional Headquarters. Officer Wong lead him into a meeting room.

"Have you been able to find anything?" asked Wah.

"No. Apart from your fingerprints on the envelope, there is nothing to find. The plastic bag only had your fingerprints on it. It must be new and the hotel employee always wears gloves. He couldn't tell how the note got into your paper. It could have been practically any hotel guest."

Wah looked at the ground. The kidnappers were extremely careful. Wah's eyes could hardly focus on one spot. Like a wild animal panicking, his eyes were constantly moving. His nerves were on edge. He didn't know how Mui was doing. Was she still alive?

"We have to go."

Inspector Cheung had pulled him out of his thoughts.

"Beg your pardon?"

"We have to go. You are to be at Po Lin Monastery at twelve o'clock. Unfortunately, since the kidnappers insist on public transport, we can't chauffeur you."

"I know."

Wah left the police station and walked to the MTR station 'Sheung Wan'. He was followed by some plainclothed police officers.

At 'Central' he boarded the next train to Tsuen Wan, which he already left again in 'Lai King' in order to change to the train to 'Tung Chung'.

29 June 2005, 10:45 am, Lantau Island, Hong Kong

The queue at the bus stop of line 23 was long. Many elderly Hong Kongers were waiting with Wah. The elderly people were mainly women. One young woman seemed to be accompanying her grandmother. A few plainclothes policemen were also in the queue. Some had arrived with him. They wore headphones and pretended to listen to music. In fact, they were able to listen to the radio communication and thus stay in contact with each other.

Then there was a group of young men. A man standing by the group, who might be around forty, with slightly longer, brown-coloured hair, ran his right hand through his hair. Wah noticed that the first limb of his middle finger was missing. 'A Triad member.' it immediately popped into his head. He looked more closely at the young men. Most of them also had dyed brown hair. Some had highlights or only dyed the upper half of their hair. They seemed to be quite young. Wah felt as if he were standing in a group of Triad recruits who were also going to Po Lin Monastery to participate in an initiation ceremony. And the man with the severed middle finger limb was their Big Brother. Wah wondered if one of all these people was one of the kidnappers.

A glance at the police officers who were supposed to be keeping an eye on Wah showed him that they thought the same. I wonder if this was a police disease, to immediately draw such conclusions? Then there was a pair of lovers in the immediate vicinity in front of him. The young man was tall and had dark red hair that reached almost to his shoulders. It was Nie Wen. He was dressed entirely in black and wore modern oval sunglasses. His supposed girlfriend was dressed in a colourful, breezy summer dress and had a small white handbag hanging from her forearm. She had hooked herself firmly onto him and was talking to him incessantly. Wah knew the young woman. It was Mei, a former colleague from the Narcotics Bureau. Wah looked at the floor. If the situation were not so serious, he would have burst out laughing.

Finally the bus arrived. A stream of visitors got off. Now there was movement in the queue. Wah was lucky because he still got a seat on the bus. Some of the young men and the man with the shortened middle finger also got on. Others were less lucky. They had to wait another thirty minutes for the next bus.

In the bus, the air conditioning was running at full blast. It drove slowly along the partly very narrow road. Every now and then the bus had to dodge oncoming vehicles. Wah sat on the left side and looked out of the window. Nie Wen and Mei sat in front of the bus. Yet he could still hear Mei's voice. He grinned. She gave an excellent portrayal of a spoilt Hong Kong woman. The other passengers were quiet.

As they drove through a village, the bus had to avoid a free-roaming ox. That was normal. Wah had almost forgotten about the ox. But he remembered that it must have always been there. Memories of a happier time came back to him. All at once he calmed down and felt some inner peace. It was as if he felt Ai

Ling's hand on his arm and heard her whisper to him. 'Don't worry, darling. You'll be fine. You're the best policeman in the whole world. You'll get those guys.' That was how she had always encouraged him when he was unsure about a case. A tear ran down his cheek. He wiped the wet trail from his face and cleared his throat.

Suddenly the bus stopped. The young men and the supposed Big Brother got out. There was a construction site here. So they were construction workers.

The bus set off again and a few minutes later Wah was standing in the grounds of Po Lin Monastery.

29 June 2005, 11:55 am, Lantau Island, Hong Kong, Po Lin Monastery

A wide variety of people gathered at the Po Lin monastery. School classes, tourists and believers. A few stray dogs were running around. Some of the believers bowed several times to the twenty-three-metre-high bronze Buddha, who was on an altar-like pedestal, looking far into the country. Some paid him the highest reverence by bowing and then lying flat on the ground. This gesture was repeated several times.

Wah went to the ticket office and bought a ticket to get to the Sitting Buddha.

"For $60 you can get a free lunch at the restaurant on top of that."

"No, thank you. A normal ticket please."

Wah took the ticket and began to climb the steps. Two hundred and sixty steps up to the Sitting Buddha. This was how Buddhists earned merit in this life for the next. Slowly, Wah climbed the stairs. It was just before twelve o'clock. He looked around attentively. Arriving at the Buddha, he entered the interior of the statue.

Inside the Buddha was a wooden staircase that led upstairs to the small museum, which kept old writings and drawings. Two employees stood at a small standing desk and checked the tickets.

On the lower level of the Buddha, which Wah had just entered, one could walk to the right and left. There were name plaques attached to the walls. Some of these plaques also had a picture on them. In front of them were tables with bowls of offerings and flowers. Wah went to the right. He looked at the name plaques. When he arrived at the table with the fourth offering bowl full of oranges, he turned around briefly. No one was paying attention to him.

He stood close to the table and lifted the bowl a little with his left hand while he searched for a note underneath with his right hand. He found it. Wah took the note and put the bowl back down. He was nervous. Where would this message lead him now?

He stepped out of the Buddha and went to the left to get out of the hustle and bustle. He leaned against the Buddha's altar and unfolded the note.

'MDME. TUSSAUDS - SMALL BLACK BAG AT TERESA TANG'

He put the piece of paper into a plastic bag. Even though he doubted that fingerprints other than his own would be found on the paper, it still had to be examined. Wah went down the stairs. He walked across the large square to a table on which lay various sized packets of incense. Wah took three medium-sized incense sticks out of a packet, lit them on the fires that were waiting and went to a container filled with sand, which already had a lot of incense sticks in it. Wah held the incense sticks in front of his face with his hands together. He closed his eyes and prayed in silence, bowed three times and put the incense sticks into the sand with his right hand while touching his right elbow with his left hand. He watched the glow of the sticks for a short while and then turned away.

He walked back to the bus stop.

Mei waited near the souvenir stalls for Nie Wen's return and watched the people walking through the square. She also saw Wah walk past her to light incense sticks. Attentively, she eyed all the people around Wah. No one seemed to be paying any attention to him. At least no one who was not part of the police force. She knew a few colleagues from Inspector Cheung's team by sight. Then she saw Nie Wen coming down the big staircase and went towards him.

Inspector Cheung also walked past the souvenir stalls. He kept glancing at the Buddha. When he saw Wah coming down the stairs, Inspector Cheung strolled to the bus stop. A few tourists stood between him and Wah. But when the bus came, Wah was able to sit down in the empty seat next to Inspector Cheung in the last row.

"What did it say?" asked Inspector Cheung quietly.

"Mdme. Tussauds - little black bag at Teresa Tang."

"Why do they go to so much trouble?"

"Psychological warfare." countered Wah wearily.

Inspector Cheung nodded. He felt sorry for Wah. Then he took out his mobile phone and sent a text message to Mary, who was sitting in the office and kept in touch with the whole team. Arrangements had to be made.

Wah looked at the area. If the brakes of the bus failed or they fell into a precipice, he would have it over with. Then this fear for Mui would not torment him any further. But he was also aware that that would be Mui's death sentence all the more. As long as he was alive, he might still be able to save her. He had to remain optimistic. At the moment, they didn't know who had something against him or where Mui was. The suspicion that the Yi Wong was behind all this could not yet be confirmed. But as soon as one of these questions was clarified, he could breathe a sigh of relief. He would no longer be condemned to react, but could finally take the initiative. Until then, he had to abide by the rules that someone was imposing on him.

29 June 2005, 13:23, Hong Kong Island, The Peak, Madame Tussauds

Wah took the ticket and went down the steps.

"Do you want a picture with Jackie?" the staff member asked him.

"No, thank you."

Wah walked past the Jackie Chan wax figure. A small queue had formed behind him.

Wah hadn't been here for a long time. At Madame Tussauds you could be close to your stars, at least those who were there as wax figures. You could stand next to the personalities from politics, sport, society, film and music and have your photo taken. There was a lot of laughter and the flashlights lit up again and again.

'Where is the figure of Teresa Tang?' Wah asked himself. He did not feel like laughing. He walked through the first room. Queen Elizabeth II, Prince Charles or Alfred Hitchcock were not his interest. 'Where is Teresa Tang?" something inside him rushed him. It was restlessness. And the hope of hearing from Mui again soon. At last. There she was: Teresa Tang.

With a braided pigtail resting over her shoulder, one hand on her hip and dressed in a colourful qipao, she smiled at him. She was standing on a small stage. Next to it was a roundel on which four of her costumes were placed. Wah looked around. He spotted a small black ladies' handbag under one of the dresses. A few guests walked past him laughing. Wah waited until he was alone again. Then he quickly bent down and picked up the handbag. He opened the clasp of the bag. A mobile phone was inside. Nothing else. Wah held his breath. On the display was a picture of Mui.

Mui looked tired and worn out. She seemed barely able to keep her eyes open and there was no longer any sign of her zest for life. Wah's eyes widened in horror. Tears came to his eyes. He took a deep breath and clutched the phone.

He put his head back slightly and had to force himself not to cry out loud. The sight of her pained him. Would he ever be able to hold Mui in his arms again? His anger at the kidnappers, however, helped him to quickly get himself under control again.

Wah walked quickly towards the exit. To his left, a large stage appeared on which Leslie Cheung was standing. Dressed in a black cheongsam. One hand placed behind his back, his left hand extended forward in an open gesture. One of his songs was playing in the background. Some guests were taking pictures of him. They looked depressed. His suicide was still incomprehensible to many.

Wah hurried on. He had to try to save the dearest thing he still owned in the world. Past the wax figure of Andy Lau. Past Anita Mui. Wah was almost running when he reached the exit.

The sultry air immediately welcomed him back as he stepped out of the Peak Tower. He walked a little way down the street. Inspector Cheung was coming towards him.

"A new message?"

"No."

Wah held up the mobile phone so that Inspector Cheung could also see the display with Mui's picture. Inspector Cheung swallowed.

"Have you been able to find out who put the handbag with the phone there?"

"Unfortunately, no. The lenses of the surveillance cameras were sprayed with paint and due to an incident it was not immediately detected."

Wah nodded slowly. They were definitely not dealing with beginners.

Suddenly the mobile phone rang.

"Hello?"

"We want fifty-eight kilograms of cocaine. - More information to follow."

Click.

Wah's hand trembled.

"What do they want?" asked Inspector Cheung.

"Fifty-eight kilograms of cocaine."

Inspector Cheung breathed in and out loudly. That was a lot of cocaine. A real fortune.

Now at least they knew what they wanted in exchange for Mui. And there was still some hope for Mui.

"Let's go to the office."

Inspector Cheung briefly put his hand on Wah's shoulder. Wah nodded. His hand clutched the mobile phone as tightly as if his own life depended on it. It was the only link to Mui at the moment.

They went to a taxi and drove back to the police station.

There were many tourists on the south terrace, opposite the Peak Tower. They walked along the railing and photographed the breathtaking view down into the skyscraper canyons of Hong Kong Island, the skyscraper-lined Victoria Bay, all the way to Kowloon. Even though it was a little hazy due to the high humidity, you could even see the mountains of the New Territories on the mainland.

There were also a few Chinese among the tourists, standing here and there in the crowd. One of the Chinese, who had a good view of the square in front of the Peak Tower, took a mobile phone out of his jacket pocket and dialled. Shortly afterwards, he heard a voice.

"How did he take it?"

"He swallowed it." the man replied.

"Police?"

"Yes."

"I thought so. - Good, go back to the flat."

The man put the mobile phone back in his jacket pocket and left the terrace.

Another Chinese man with dark red, shoulder-length hair had been standing next to him. He was wearing headphones and had taken a photo of the Peak Tower. When the former turned away and walked towards the exit, Nie Wen turned around and took his picture. Nie Wen then switched off the listening device, plugged the headphones into his MP3 player and walked himself towards the exit, making way for a group of Australian tourists.

30 June 2005, 8:48 a.m., Hong Kong Island, HKPF Crime Wing HK Island Regional Headquarters

Wah was sitting in Inspector Cheung's office and had handed him a list of the Yi Wong's properties.

"Where did you get the list?" asked Inspector Cheung.

"From an informant."

"And you're sure your informant didn't pull any crap on you?"

"Yes."

Inspector Cheung turned back to the two lists on his desk. The list his team had compiled and the list Wah had handed over were mostly in agreement. The few additional properties that were not on the police list had already been marked by Inspector Cheung. One of them was near the Novotel Century Harbourview where Wah was staying.

"So you really think Wong would be crazy enough to hide the girl there?" asked Wong.

"It would have some points of security for the kidnappers. They'll also be able to figure out that we're getting a list of the properties. And normally you'd assume the furthest, least accessible property."

"But the kidnappers also know which hotel you are in and therefore also that you live nearby. Why would Wong Wei Yan be so crazy to hide Mui there of all places?"

"Either he thinks it's an extra thrill or he just assumes that we don't even know that he owns this flat. And therefore feels safe."

Cheung leaned back in his chair.

"I will discuss this with the team later. - Is there anything else on your mind?"

"Where did you get the Yi Wong payroll?" asked Wah.

"Ah! You found it. - Was it too obvious?"

"It was impossible to miss."

"Well, as you are so stubborn regarding Nie Wen. We thought you wouldn't believe a word we said."

"I'm not sure even now."

"Why? Isn't that clear enough yet?"

"How long has he been on it?"

"We don't know that."

"Who gave you the list?"

"From an informant. Just like you." Inspector Cheung grinned at Wah.

"But probably not from the same one." Wah remarked dryly. The grin on Inspector Cheung's face disappeared.

"Why do you still not believe us?"

"Did you know that Nie Wen Wong is Wei Yan's half-brother?"

"Beg your pardon?!"

"Nie Wen is the illegitimate son of Wong Zhao Wen, Wong Wei Yan's father."

"Since when do you know that?"

"Since I investigated Wong Zhao Wen. At first I was horrified. I had him under surveillance, had put out some decoys. Nothing happened. Nie Wen didn't respond to a single one. He only knew Wong Zhao Wen as the Chairman of Yi Wong. Otherwise he had no contact with him at all."

"What makes you so sure of that?"

"Wong Zhao Wen had made a good decision once in his life. His illegitimate son should not come into contact with the Yi Wong and he had even invisibly supported Nie Wen when he wanted to go to the police."

"Why is that?"

"He had loved Nie Wen's mother excessively. But she never wanted to have anything to do with Wong's business. Always kept the son away from Wong. Yet, he pulled the strings from afar."

"How do you know all this?"

"I learned this from Wong himself. When he was hit in the shootout, his people surrendered shortly afterwards. I went to him. He died in my arms. He made me promise that Nie Wen would never know. Yan probably hadn't made such a promise, or thought he didn't have to keep it."

"Does Nie Wen know that you know?"

"I don't think so. - I had a hacker check it. Nie Wen has only one account. The amount supposedly going to Nie Wen is going into another man's account. The list has been manipulated."

"Probably the account is not under his real name." Inspector Cheung said.

Wah shook his head.

"No. Not under any other name and not in

Switzerland, not in the Channel Islands, not in the Caribbean. Nowhere. He has only one account and it is by no means brimming with wealth. The amount on your payroll goes to another man. I've already checked."

With these words, Wah handed the inspector a piece of paper with the name of the person in question written on it.

"Why are you doing this?"

"I simply cannot sit idly in my hotel room and wait, Inspector. I can't! I want my daughter back!"

"We are working on it, Wah. We are working on it. But don't do anything on your own. That can do Mui more harm than good."

"Have you been able to find out who sent the text message with the number?" changed Wah the subject.

"Sent from the Internet. The computer is located at Pacific Coffee, Tsim Sha Tsui."

"Any information from a CCTV?"

"No, the one in question wore a cap and sunglasses. We could see that he came from the Western District, but that's it. All the way the face was not visible. No chance to identify him."

"They're fucking careful." uttered Wah.

"One way to put it. - In the meantime, do you have any idea what the number '72' could mean?"

"The only thing I can think of is the anniversary of our operation against the Yi Wong. The 2nd of July."

"I had already thought of that. That would be in

two days... In just over forty-eight hours."

"No," Wah began thoughtfully. "In seventy-two hours."

Inspector Cheung looked at him questioningly.

"I got the message yesterday at 8 p.m.. So Wong will probably schedule the handover on 2 July at 8 p.m.."

Inspector Cheung tilted his head.

"Why 8 p.m.?"

"At 8 p.m. on 2 July 1998, the doctor diagnosed the death of Wong Zhao Wen."

Wah became restless. That was what he had needed. A clue. Now, at last, he knew the time. He could prepare himself for that. The wait would soon be over.

"Inspector, we must find Mui! I doubt Wong will hand her over to me. He wants to take *revenge* on me. The cocaine is just a nice addition. By 8 p.m., the doctor had diagnosed Wong Zhao Wen's death. And Yan is probably planning that this will also be my time of death. Or worse, Mui's."

Wah shivered at the thought.

"We will prevent that, Wah. Let's first get the delivery of the sample over with tonight. After that, I'll discuss the next steps with the team."

"I want to be at the meeting."

"No."

"I'm a policeman!"

"No."

"After all, it's about my daughter!"

"And that is exactly why you will stay away and let us do our job! You already do enough on the side."

Tung could be stubborn, Cheung as well.

"Wah, be reasonable. You could endanger everything. I know you are an excellent policeman and have received some awards. But you are too emotionally involved in this case. Please don't do anything rash. For your daughter's sake."

Wah pressed his lips together and stood up to go to the door. He knew Cheung was right. But he was also a father, as Cheung had aptly pointed out.

30 June 2005, 10:00 am, Hong Kong Island, Pok Fu Lam, Cemetery

Wah had not been here for seven years. The risk of being recognised was too great. It was quiet in this place. Despite the fact that Pok Fu Lam Road ran above the cemetery. Birds were chirping. Every now and then, the call of an osprey could be heard. Just before Nie Wen reached him, Wah turned to him.

"Hello."

"Hello."

Nie Wen stood next to Wah and saw that Wah had placed a bunch of white lilies on the grave. Ai Ling's favourite flowers.

"Thank you for helping the in-laws with the grave maintenance."

"Don't mention it. - Have you spoken to them yet?" asked Nie Wen.

"No. Not since the funeral. My father-in-law won't speak to me again until I have avenged her death."

"They miss Ai Ling very much. But they also miss Mui and you."

"Mui writes to them regularly." Wah fell silent. Then he said softly, "Wrote...".

"She'll do it again, Wah."

Both men were silent. Too many questions hung in the air. But who could answer them all. Who knew the truth? Truth. Was there one truth? No. There was no *one truth.* But who knew at least *the* fraction of truth that would have helped Wah?

"Is there any news?" Nie Wen interrupted the

silence. Wah closed his eyes briefly. Had Nie Wen betrayed him? Had he betrayed Mui?

"The police have a list of all the Yi Wong properties."

"The only question is whether *all the* Yi Wong properties are really on there."

"The list is from the Yi Wong themselves."

"What?"

Wah smiled.

"Who did you have to kill for that?" teased Nie Wen, trying to mask his surprise.

Wah had had an informant at the Yi Wong before. Until today, Nie Wen had not been able to find out who it was.

"Did you find out anything?" Wah asked him.

"No. No one knows anything about a kidnapped girl. Nothing unusual happened at the monastery. There was no one observing you that I could have followed. - Sorry I'm not much help."

Nie Wen was depressed. He would have liked to tell Wah about the trail he followed, but thought it wiser to remain silent for the time being.

"Have the kidnappers contacted you again?"

"Yes. I was passed a mobile phone at Madame Tussauds."

Wah took the mobile phone out of his pocket and showed Nie Wen the picture of the exhausted Mui that was on the display.

"Shit!"

"They want fifty-eight kilograms of cocaine in

exchange for Mui."

"Are the police joining in?"

"What else. Where else would I be able to procure so much cocaine in a short time?!"

"When is it going to take place?"

"I don't know yet. I have to wait until they get back to me."

"Have you looked at the list?" asked Nie Wen.

"What list?"

"Well, the one with the properties."

"I skimmed over them. Why?"

"Did you find anything where Mui might be hiding?"

"About three dozen." replied Wah quietly.

"Nothing the police are speculating on the most?"

Wah was silent. He was exhausted and burnt out. The fact that he no longer knew whether he could continue to trust his best friend also sapped his strength. Even though he was sure that the *evidence* against Nie Wen was fabricated. Nevertheless, he became more and more cautious towards Nie Wen. On the one hand, this made him ashamed, on the other hand, it made him angry. Too many questions were unanswered. Besides, he was worried about Mui. His daughter had done nothing to anyone and had to atone just because she was his daughter.

Nie Wen seemed to have guessed his thoughts, because he asked him straight out.

"Since when do you know?"

"What?"

Wah now turned completely to Nie Wen.

"That Wong Zhao Wen was my father?"

"Since my investigation of him."

"And why did you keep me involved?"

"No one else knew. Not even you. You had no contact with him or the Yi Wong."

"Where from..."

"I had you shadowed."

Wah smiled wanly.

Nie Wen snorted briefly. He had thought something like that.

"You are Yan's half-brother. Why didn't you prevent the kidnapping?"

Wah looked reproachfully at Nie Wen.

"I don't think he knows."

"What? That he's your half-brother? - Don't take me for a fool. You work for the Yi Wong."

"I'm an errand boy. He has used me from time to time. But I doubt he knows who I am."

"Why didn't you stop the kidnapping?"

"It was not publicly announced in the Yi Wong Bulletin that Tung Ming Wah's daughter was to be kidnapped." Nie Wen remarked flippantly.

"Who are you?" asks Wah, quivering with anger.

"I'm still the same."

"No. Not for a long time."

"Then why do you still trust me?"

"Do I?"

"Would you talk to me otherwise?"

"At a distance, I couldn't tell how much you had changed. From a policeman to a gangster!" said Wah snidely.

"There are far more things in life than you can imagine," Nie Wen remarked dryly.

"Are you really a private detective? Or is that a lie too?"

"Hoho!!!! That's enough, Wah! I'm not a liar. And yes, I am a private detective. Even if I am employed by the Yi Wong from time to time."

"So occasionally deployed is what you call it."

"Yes, deployed from time to time. - I haven't changed sides, Wah! On the contrary. It is the Yi Wong who has changed sides."

Nie Wen would have loved to punch his friend in the jaw. But what good would it have done? Nothing at all. Wah knew only the smallest fraction of what Nie Wen was really doing. And he couldn't let him in on the other part. It was too dangerous. For him and for Wah, as well as for Ai Mui. So Nie Wen tried to smooth things over a little.

"I didn't know anything about a kidnapping!"

"Do you know where she is?"

"No, otherwise you'd have her back by now."

"He doesn't trust you?"

"I've already told you that he probably doesn't know. I'm just a little light. In one of the lowest levels."

"Are you in?"

Nie Wen rolled his eyes. It was not reasonable to talk to Wah at the moment.

"No. I am not one of the kidnappers."

Wah looked at his watch.

"Do you have a date?"

Wah nodded.

"I'll let you know if I find out anything, Wah! You'll just have to trust me. If you can still trust me. Maybe I can help after all."

"We'll see."

Their paths parted. The friendship of the past no longer existed. It had a crack.

30 June 2005, 13:05, Hong Kong Island, Wan Chai, Wan Chai Road

A waitress came up to Yan. "Good afternoon." she said, bowing slightly to him.

"Good afternoon," Yan replied. "I have an appointment with Dai Lou Chan."

The young woman's posture stiffened a little.

"Who may I report?"

"Wong Wei Yan."

"One moment please."

The waitress walked through the restaurant. Yan looked around the room. The large round tables were almost all full. The buzz of voices was mixed with laughter here and there. The waitress appeared in his field of vision again and walked towards him.

"Mr Wong, Dai Lou Chan is expecting you. - Please come."

Yan nodded his head briefly and followed her down the hall. The waitress opened a door at the back of the hall and Yan stepped through. The waitress closed the door behind him.

Yan found himself in a narrow hallway. A tall Chinese man in a black suit walked towards him. A second, very strong one followed him.

"Mr Wong?"

"Yes."

"We have to search you. Please understand."

The suit-wearer took out a metal detector like those used at airports, among other places. Yan had to stretch out his arms. The man's hand followed the metal detectors so that he could also feel that the visit could not be dangerous to the boss in any way. After finding nothing except a fountain pen and a wallet with ID cards and credit cards, he turned to the strongly built man.

"It's all right." he said.

He stepped aside and let Yan pass. Yan was now between the two and followed him. Mr Chan was very careful.

They climbed the tiled stairs to the second floor. Once there, a door was opened so that they could enter a large room.

The room had small windows facing the courtyard. It was very simply designed. Work was clearly being done here. In a corner to Yan's right was a small laboratory. Drugs were probably tested there for their quality. To his left was a large round table with a large teapot in the middle. An elderly gentleman in a grey suit sat in the middle, to his right and left sat a total of five employees. In front of the elderly gentleman was a teacup. A second teacup was on an unoccupied seat directly opposite. The two Chinese who had brought Yan took seats on the chairs next to the door.

Yan memorised all the details in seconds. Meanwhile, the elderly gentleman stood up. He was somewhat obese and had very short-cropped hair. Yan estimated him to be in his early fifties. He had seen him from time to time at meetings where his father had taken him. Which was rare, though. But he had never had any closer contact with Mr Chan.

With a broad smile and outstretched arms, Mr Chan walked towards Yan.

"Wong Wei Yan!" he exclaimed delightedly.

His voice was rough and sounded a little shrill.

"How nice to finally welcome you to my humble office."

"Thank you very much, Dai Lou Chan."

Mr Chan asked Yan to sit down and led him to the place in front of the second teacup.

"I have to excuse my caution. But at the moment things have become very turbulent in the industry and I don't want to take any risks."

"Understandable."

"Would you like some tea?"

This was more of a rhetorical question, as he gestured to a staff member to pour Yan tea.

"Thank you very much."

Mr Chan went back to his seat.

"I've heard a lot about you." began Mr Chan, looking challengingly at Yan.

The atmosphere in the room seemed almost surreal to Yan. On the surface, one might have thought it was a meeting with a fatherly friend. But Yan knew how powerful and dangerous Mr Chan was. He was a confidant of one of Hong Kong's greatest Dragon Heads. Yan had to be very careful. He had already heard too much about the already legendary Dai Lou Chan.

"You were on holiday, I heard."

Chan smiled at Yan. It was a knowing smile. A cold

smile.

"Yes, I was visiting my friend in London."

Yan looked Dai Lou Chan straight in the eye. Mr Chan nodded slightly and took a sip of tea.

"I haven't been to London for a long time," Mr Chan began. "Chinatown used to be nice. But these days it seems to be on the verge of selling out."

"It has changed a lot just in the time from my studies until now. And yet you can still sense the former glamour and bustle of those days."

Mr Chan seemed satisfied with the statement. But that was not why he had sent for Yan.

"At the moment it is also very busy there again. - Unfortunately not the way we would like it to be."

Yan immediately picked up on the hypothermic tone.

"The news is full of reports about the many raids and arrests."

Yan thus dared to step forward. He could not pretend to be ignorant. They would never buy it, it would only increase suspicion against him. Hopefully he would not turn Mr. Chan against him. Mr Chan's eyebrows drew together. Yan had caught the ball that had been thrown to him.

"Do you know more details?" asked Mr Chan.

"No. Only what is reported in the news."

"They say you saw the dead man that day - alive."

"It was only when a picture came on the news that I knew who it was. He could neither be missed nor overheard in the restaurant. My table was on the opposite side."

Mr Chan took a sip of tea to wash down his rising anger.

"At the moment, many members of our families have problems with the police. Some of them were just able to get home."

Mr Chan paused for a moment before continuing.

"This is not good for business. We will be disrupted in our work. If we are not careful, other syndicates will take care of our business in London. But what am I burdening you with my grief. - After all, you were only visiting your friend in London."

Now Yan also took a sip of tea. His throat felt as if it were parched. He knew it was a threat. But he didn't know why Dai Lou Chan was talking to him about it. Or rather: even seemed to suspect him.

"If I can be of any use to you..." offered Yan.

"I am sure that we will find the perpetrators of this unrest. But I thank you for the offer. - It's always good to have someone who can bring people to Hong Kong – nearly unnoticed."

Yan frowned for a split second. But then he smiled, raised his cup and toasted Mr Chan across the table.

Mr Chan had seen the brief movement and the look on Yan's face. His suspicions had been confirmed.

Nie Wen had followed Yan to Mr Chan's restaurant. He sat down at a table in the small cookshop opposite the restaurant and waited. A foreigner entered. He was far too well dressed to be eating in a cookshop. The man ordered his food in perfect Cantonese. As he turned to go to an empty table, the foreigner noticed Nie Wen and stared for a brief moment. Then he moved on and sat down at a table behind Nie Wen.

Nie Wen took a sip of his milk tea. This was the same foreigner as in the Municipal Centre a few days ago. And the foreigner also seemed to be at the cookshop for the same reason as Nie Wen.

To observe the building opposite. The building where Wong Wei Yan was currently staying.

30 June 2005, 14:55, Hong Kong Island, Queens Road West

Wah quietly closed the door. He wore gloves so he wouldn't leave any fingerprints. Always on the alert for surprises, he checked the bedroom, the kitchen and the small bathroom. Nie Wen was not there. Wah relaxed a little. He took a glass from the sink and placed it on the handle of the flat door. If someone came in, the breaking of the glass would at least warn him.

In the bedroom, Wah had seen that there were a few pieces of clothing on the floor. The wardrobe and the chest of drawers had been emptied. So Nie Wen had been in a hurry. Because normally it was always extremely tidy in his house. Was he on the run? If so, from whom?

Wah opened the cupboard doors in the living room. Folders. Neatly labelled: assignments. A folder for each year. Wah leafed through a few folders. Mostly it was runaway animals, occasionally lost or stolen objects. Then came a file box containing names and addresses of clients. Then folders again. This time with bank statements. Wah took out the folders. The same numbers he had already seen.

When Wah pulled another folder out of the cupboard, the blueprint of a building fell to the floor of the cupboard. It had been behind the folders. Wah picked up the blueprint. He looked for the address and widened his eyes when he found it. It was the building where Mui was believed to be. Wah's breath caught in his throat. Had Nie Wen been involved in the kidnapping after all?

Wah's head began to spin. He felt sick with anger when suddenly the mobile phone Nie Wen had given him rang.

"Hello."

"Get out of my flat!" Nie Wen shouted excitedly into the phone.

"What do you have to do with the kidnapping?"

"Get out of my flat!"

"Where is Mui?" roared Wah.

"Get out of the flat or you won't be able to do anything with the answers! Out! *Now!* "

Nie Wen hung up. He stood at the window with his binoculars and watched Wah. Fortunately, Wah had taken the warning seriously and ran out of Nie Wen's field of vision. Nie Wen was nervous. Hopefully Wah would still make it in time.

As Wah left the flat, he could already hear someone running loudly up the stairs. The lifts were in motion. Wah tried to run as quietly as possible to the stairs. At the first landing, he quickly took off his shoes and then ran up the stairs on socks. Below him he heard some voices shouting, then something cracked. Wah continued to run upwards. Finally he reached the roof. Completely out of breath, Wah put his shoes back on and looked around. Several terraces were connected at different heights by fire escapes. All of them were surrounded by high metal grates. Then Wah spotted the guttering, most of which ran along beside the excellent windows of the flats. That was his only chance. Lift or stairs were too dangerous for him.

Wah went to the small terrace that closed off next to the gutter. The crossbar of the grating was connected to another edge. At a distance of about one metre. But its edge was connected to the gutter. Wah wondered again if he might not be discovered then, by whoever Nie Wen had warned him about. No, the window ledges would hide him. So there was nothing to fear. At least not in that respect.

Wah pulled himself up the bars of the lattice until he reached the bordering crossbar. He carefully pushed himself up with his arms and placed his feet on the crossbar. Very slowly. He could not lose his balance under any circumstances. He looked down for a moment. It was far more than twenty storeys down.

'But you're not supposed to look down, you're always supposed to look up,' Wah thought, to give himself courage. In front of him was the iron bar that formed the outer edge. Level with his feet. Wah counted to three and grabbed the bar with both hands. A second later he was hanging high above the precipice and slowly worked his way down, fully relying on the strengths of his hands. His feet made contact with the gutter. Then he could also reach for it with his hands. He pressed his forehead against the cool metal.

He had to be crazy. But there was no turning back now. Only a 'down'. And how this 'down' went now depended entirely on his concentration, his will and his muscles. Slowly, very slowly, he let himself slide down. As soon as he could reach one of the protruding windows with his feet, he rested briefly, relaxed his hands. He was still wearing the gloves and he was glad of it.

"That crazy guy." Nie Wen said almost tonelessly when he spotted Wah on the roof of the building. Partly horrified, partly admiring, Nie Wen watched Wah slowly lower himself down the gutter. Every now and then Nie Wen turned back to his flat. The men were still at it. Nie Wen got goose bumps. Glad that his instincts had not betrayed him. He looked back over at Wah, who had already passed the upper half of the building. That was when Nie Wen noticed the men on the roof. They were searching the terraces. But no one thought to look down. Luckily for Wah.

Ten minutes later, which seemed like an eternity to Wah, he was able to let go of the gutter and fell about two metres to the floor of an intermediate roof that could be used by the residents. Relieved but physically exhausted, he leaned against the wall. His muscles ached, he was sweaty, his lungs burned as if he had run a marathon and his knees were shaking.

Only after some time did he feel well enough to walk away. He went to the stairwell. Quietly he opened the door. There was silence. He ran down the stairs of the last floor, trying not to be too loud. At the bottom, he carefully opened the door. Passers-by and a few tourists walked leisurely past him. Wah took off his gloves, patted his jeans a little and stepped out onto the street in an upright posture. He immediately melted into the crowd.

Nie Wen had been waiting at the street corner for Wah to appear and followed him. Now it was time to act before the situation got completely out of control.

30 June 2005, 15:28, Hong Kong Island, HKPF Crime Wing HK Island Regional Headquarters

Mary entered Inspector Cheung's office.

"Tung was called by Chow earlier."

"Well?"

"Tung was at Chow's flat and Chow was at the Novotel."

"You gotta be kidding me."

"No, sir. He did, and Chow even checked in with his real name."

Cheung leaned back. What kind of topsy-turvy world was this that he was in at the moment?

"It gets better," Mary began cautiously.

Cheung rubbed his eyes. He could hardly wait to close this case.

"Shoot." he said, annoyed.

"Chow must have watched Tung and warned him that there were probably some thugs on their way to the flat."

"Chow was watching his own flat?"

"Seems so."

"Go on."

"Tung was smart enough to take this warning seriously. He was seen appearing on the roof, climbing over the terrace barrier and then lowering himself down the gutter."

Inspector Cheung started laughing.

"It's like an action movie in here." He raised his hand apologetically. "Go on."

"Er, yes, it must have been something like that. At least someone called the police that a man was climbing down the gutter by the building."

"Where are they now?"

"We don't know. Chow seems to have switched off his mobile phone when he left the hotel. And according to our tracker, Tung is in his hotel room. But he's not there."

"What about the kidnappers' phone? He's hardly likely to have switched that off."

Mary cleared her throat. "Well, he did."

"Damn." Cheung sat back. This couldn't be true. Tung wasn't stupid. He knew he had to remain accessible to the kidnappers....

"Mary, check with the provider to see if a forwarding has been set up. And then check with the new number to see where he is. He *must be* reachable for the kidnappers!"

"Will do immediately, sir."

"Send someone to Chow's flat. I want to know what happened there."

"Yes, sir."

When Mary had left the office, Inspector Cheung sat up straight and rubbed his palms firmly over his face. At first he had feared that Tung had blown a fuse. But according to this information, he still seemed to be able to think clearly. Well, like one could climb down a gutter thinking clearly. Tung seemed to have a plan. But what was it? And why should thugs be sent after Chow? Was he not one of the kidnappers? But why would Wong Wei Yan want to get rid of him? And where the hell was Tung at the moment?

"We'll get you, friend," Cheung said quietly to himself.

30 June 2005, 15:35, Hong Kong Island

Inspector Choi and his assistant, Chan Mei Ling, entered the high-rise building and took the lift to the eighth floor. The colleagues from the forensics department were already on the scene and taking pictures. Choi and Mei Ling could already see that a fight had taken place when they entered the flat. The iron-like smell of blood was also in the air. The smell was only intensified by the high humidity in Hong Kong. In the living room, they immediately saw the corpse.

His hands, feet and head had been cut off and placed next to his body. Choi first looked around.

"14K?" said Mei Ling, cocking her head to one side.

"Maybe."

"I'd like to know what he revealed." Mei Ling thought aloud.

Choi looked at her briefly with raised eyebrows, shook his head and then went to the body to get a first picture of it.

"Nice." the coroner remarked dryly as he entered the living room behind the two and discovered the body.

Choi turned around.

"Hello doctor."

"What has this guy done wrong?" the doctor asked.

"You can team up with Mei Ling on that. She would also like to know what information he passed on," Choi countered.

"Don't you want to know?"

"I just want to know *who did* this and catch them."

The doctor turned to Mei Ling.

"He's been around too long."

Mei Ling grinned and shrugged her shoulders briefly. Choi turned to a police officer.

"Have you been able to find out anything yet?"

"The murdered man was known as Johnny Lee. Unfortunately, we have not been able to find out more about him in the short time we have had. The neighbour vis-à-vis this aparment said something about a man who was there last night. There must have been a fight. My colleague is taking the statement now."

"I understand."

Somehow he had a hunch that this case was connected to another case. He just couldn't make sense of how it would be if his suspicions were confirmed.

"Well, I'll get your report," he turned back to the police officer.

"Of course."

After Choi had looked around carefully, he went to Mei Ling, who was standing in the living room and had made a lot of notes and also made smaller sketches. He looked over her shoulder.

After a short pause, he turned back to Mei Ling.

"Have you looked at everything?"

"I sketched a few things briefly and wrote down exactly where everything was and how to find what."

"Our colleagues at the Identification Bureau are already doing that."

"But I want it too."

"What do you think happened here?" he asked her.

"Death of a traitor."

"That's obvious."

"It hasn't been long. Only a few hours."

"Oh, you studied forensic medicine too?"

Mei Ling ignored his remark.

"Besides, it was two fights."

"Hm. "

"When he was surprised by the chop team, they had dragged him from the front door into the living room. In the process, he had lost one of the flip-flops."

"You noticed the flip-flop?"

Choi grinned.

"Then he was pushed onto the floor in the living room. They gagged him and put tape over his mouth so he couldn't scream. Then his hands and feet were cut off. The tape was only taken off later, when the head had already been cut off."

"What makes you think that?"

"After the onset of death, the entire musculature first goes limp. If you had taken the tape off him beforehand, he would have had a different facial expression. So you must have waited longer before taking the tape off him."

After a short pause, she continued.

"Besides, he would have screamed very loud. But

he didn't, because he just couldn't. I bet the interviews with the neighbours confirm that."

Choi nodded. Mei Ling had only been his assistant for a few months, but her sharp mind, quick thinking and memory, as well as her analytical skills, were simply amazing.

The coroner, who had also heard Mei Ling's explanations, turned to them.

"Choi, how did you get this woman?" he complimented the remarks.

Choi straightened his shoulders with pride and grinned.

"If you're tired of homicide, come see me, Miss Chan."

Mei Ling suppressed a giggle and nodded her thanks to the doctor. Choi's shoulders were back in their usual position, the smile gone.

"Are you finally done with the notes?" asked Choi.

"Yes."

"All right, let's go back to the office. - Doctor, when can we expect your report?"

"When I'm done. - If it's going to be tonight, you'll have to buy me a beer."

"A beer it is. You say when and where. And I have the report tonight."

The doctor laughed and waved it off.

As Choi and Mei Ling rode down in the lift, Choi checked again.

"Why two fights?"

Mei Ling had just put her notepad, which she carried around with her all the time, into the large shoulder bag and turned to him.

"Well, didn't you notice the picture frames on the wall that had fallen down and were hanging crooked in places?"

"It could have been longer."

"Not when you look at the bright patches on the wall where the pictures had hung before."

"What else?"

"The broken nose of Johnny Lee. That was still fresh, but not from the chop team. The nose had already been treated."

"Who could that have been?"

The lift door opened and they stepped out and walked to Inspector Choi's car.

"Someone who wanted the information that Johnny Lee would have been better off not giving out."

"Hopefully we can find out quite quickly who he was working for. Maybe that will help us."

"It's a pity we don't have a complete file on police informants."

"You mean a policeman broke his nose?"

"It must have been something big. Otherwise the syndicate wouldn't have reacted so strongly to it, but first inflicted first-degree cuts on him or chopped off one or two fingers at most. But to act like that straight away. That was a punishment and at the same time a warning to other members. It must be something big."

"Okay, let's find out what's going on with the colleagues at the moment. - Well observed, Mei Ling."

"Thank you, sir!"

30 June 2005, 19:51, Kowloon, Tsim Sha Tsui, Avenue of the Stars

People were already gathering. Some sat on the benches, others leaned against the railing that bordered the Avenue of the Stars towards Victoria Bay. A few photographers were setting up their tripods. The Star Cruiser "Pisces" pulled in. It was already dark. After the announcement was made that the "Symphony of Lights" would begin at 8 p.m., Mozart's "Little Night Music" sounded from the loudspeakers.

Wah sat on one of the benches and waited. The last few hours had been eventful. And exhausting. A black eye, a few bruises and abrasions, and a split lip were evidence of that. When Wah had appeared in Inspector Cheung's office half an hour earlier, the latter had almost been struck.

The climbing action had already infuriated Inspector Cheung, but that Wah now had to fight as well - because it was obvious - that was too much. But no matter how hard he tried to get answers out of Wah with questions and threats, he was unsuccessful. Wah remained silent. When it was time to leave for the Avenue of the Stars, Inspector Cheung gave up – deeply regretting that he had not been the person who punched Wah. But time was of the essence.

The game was not over yet. But the cards were reshuffled.

Finally, all the lights went out. The Symphony of Lights began. A woman's voice introduced, in three languages, each of the nineteen buildings participating in the laser show. Each building gave a small sample. Four minutes later, the real show began. White and green laser beams were also sent into the sky from some buildings. It was quite impressive how all these buildings were illuminated. But Wah could not enjoy the spectacle. He was too agitated. Too much had happened in the last few hours. He had to pull himself together so that he didn't mess up the handover now.

As he was required to do, Wah took a cigarette packet out of his jacket pocket, took out a cigarette and lit it. He took a deep drag. While Wah was smoking the cigarette, a man with a newspaper tucked under his left arm approached him.

"Could you help me out with a cigarette?"

Wah looked at the cigarette in silence for a while. Then he handed the pack to the man.

"I'm just about to quit."

"Then take something to read, it will distract you."

The cigarette packet and the newspaper changed hands. The man went on and Wah finished the cigarette quietly.

After 15 minutes the laser show was over. The crowd dispersed. Wah remained seated. After a good while, he got up and went to the nearest dustbin. He threw the newspaper into it. Only a note placed inside was important to him. Wah left the Avenue of the Stars in the direction of the bell tower and boarded the ferry to Hong Kong Island.

Followed by two policemen.

30 June 2005, 20:36, Hong Kong Island, 41D Stubbs Road, Highcliff

"Good evening, Ruby. Nice to see you again! I hope you are well." Robert greeted the older woman who had opened the door. The elderly lady smiled at him and took a step aside so that Robert could enter. Already Yan was coming towards him.

"Welcome!" Yan welcomed Robert joyfully.

"Come on, I'll give you a tour on my flat first."

Robert started to laugh. Irritated, Yan looked at him.

"What is it?"

"You're all fired up."

"Sure. I want to show you my latest acquisitons," Yan replied.

That was more the answer of a little boy than that of a syndicate Chairman.

"If I told anyone in London that I was having dinner on the sixty-seventh floor, they would think I was crazy". Robert remarked.

"They don't know how great the view is up here either. I can see over the whole of Happy Valley and even over Wan Chai". Yan announced proudly.

Yan went down a step that led into the living area. At the large window front stood a rattan seating area with white cushions. Surrounded on the left and right by large planters. There were small tables next to the sofa with various magazines and newspapers on them.

"My little island." Yan introduced his living room.

"There's nothing better than sitting comfortably in one of the sofas with a beer or a red wine and enjoying the illuminated city."

Robert could imagine that very well. What he had seen so far showed that Yan had furnished the flat for himself. It was not about showing off his status to guests. It was all about the cosiness. Extremely rare for a Hong Konger.

Yan was much more of an English man than a Hong Konger, Robert thought.

To the left of the living area stood an oak wood dining furniture. It consisted of a round table, four chairs and two heavy sideboards against the wall. The table was already set for Yan and Robert.

Yan led Robert to his study.

"Here's my office."

Robert looked around. The room was quite large and simply furnished. A desk made of wood and glass. Behind it was a leather desk chair. On the wall were two large, framed calligraphies with blessings for luck, wealth and a long life. Otherwise, the room contained a small seating area made of white leather, a low lacquer table and two antique Chinese bookshelves.

"No wonder you like working so much," Robert remarked. "What's behind the door?"

"The third bathroom."

Robert looked at Yan for a moment.

"Well, it was already furnished that way," he replied with a grin. "Come on, I'll show you the guest room. Maybe you'll want to spend the night with me after all."

They left the study. Yan carefully closed the door behind him.

The flat didn't seem to want to stop. Yan told Robert a lot about the building. About the beginning of the construction in 2000, the completion in 2003, as well as the special features of the wind dampers, which were used in this building for the first time in the world for a residential building, so that the typhoons of late summer could not harm this narrow building.

Later, Yan and Robert sat at the table and had dinner.

"How was your day today?" asked Yan, noticing that Robert was unusually quiet this evening.

Robert took a sip of wine and washed down the last mouthful with it.

"I went bowling."

"You can't go bowling every day!" Yan exclaimed.

"Why not? Here I have more peace and quiet to practise my swing. - You can come with me sometime."

"Is my name Lau Tak Wah?"

The Asian superstar's enthusiasm for bowling was well known.

"You don't know how much fun it can be. - Well, I'd like to play with Lau Tak Wah sometime. I hear he's very good. That would be a challenge." Robert responded to Yan's comment.

"Shall I arrange a game between you?"

Robert started to laugh.

"What is it?" asked Yan, slightly irritated.

"You should have asked me that a few days ago." Robert replied reproachfully.

"Why?"

"Yesterday he had bowled with the other tigers Felix and Miu. Then I would have met them altogether."

"How do you know?"

"Say, don't you read the papers?"

Yan rolled his eyes.

"Why don't you just find yourself a girl? You're not in a monastery here. Tell me which girl you like and I'll get her for you. Go shopping, take her out to a restaurant, ..."

Robert waved it off.

"Thanks, but you don't have to get me a girl. I don't feel like it either."

"And what are you in the mood for?"

But Robert no longer had time to answer. Yan's mobile phone rang.

"Excuse me a moment, please." said Yan after looking at the display. He stood up and went to his study.

Robert leaned back. His right hand played with the glass at the table while being pensive. Soon it was time to act.

Ten minutes later, Yan entered the dining room again. He looked agitated.

"Are you all right?"

"No, not really."

Yan ran his hand through his short hair. He hoped that Robert did not see that his hand was trembling with excitement.

"Just some business," Yan said, trying to smile.

They were silent for a while until Robert spoke up.

"Yan, I have to go back to London."

Yan looked at him in surprise.

"My father has sent me a message that he wishes to see me immediately."

Robert made a regretful face.

"Gone is the rest and bowling." remarked Yan. "When do you want to fly?"

"I hope to get a seat in the plane tomorrow afternoon."

"Then you'll miss the party on Saturday. What a pity. I would have liked to introduce you to some interesting men," and with a slightly bitter undertone Yan added, "we all have to make sacrifices for our fathers. That's the way it is."

"Yes, that's the way it is," Robert repeated.

"Do you know approximately how long he will require your help?"

"Not exactly. Depends on the status of negotiations. But I hope to be back here by the end of next week." Robert assured.

Yan raised his glass of wine and said with a bitter undertone, "To our fathers!"

30 June 2005, 21:00, Hong Kong Island, HKPF Crime Wing HK Island Regional Headquarters

"We have an addition." Inspector Cheung greeted the team as he entered the meeting room with Inspector Choi and Mei Ling.

"May I introduce Inspector Choi from the Homicide Department and his assistant Chan Mei Ling."

Inspector Choi and Mei Ling greeted their colleagues and took their seats at the meeting table.

"It turns out that there is a connection between a murder case Inspector Choi is working on today and our case. So we're having this joint briefing now to share our knowledge and hopefully help each other. Maybe we'll be able to put a few more pieces of the puzzle together."

The team looked curiously at each other and then at the two guests. Their case had taken an interesting turn.

"I'll start with a brief version of our case," Inspector Cheung began. "For that, I have to go back a few years.

"On 2 July 1998, a Narcotics Bureau team, on the instructions of Inspector Tung Ming Wah, strikes at a drug transfer from the Yi Wong syndicate. Tung had been investigating the Yi Wong for months and was finally able to strike. Unfortunately, gun battle ensued. To the detriment of Wong Zhao Wen, the Chairman of the Yi Wong, who had personally participated in the deal, and was shot dead. His son Wong Wei Yan became the new Chairman of Yi Wong.

He blamed Tung for his father's death and put a price on Tung's head. Tung had to go into hiding. He moved to London with his daughter, Tung Ai Mui, nickname Mui, and worked for the Metropolitan Police.

"On 16 June 2005, Tung Ming Wah was having lunch with an informant. He had noticed two men looking directly at him as they left the restaurant. One of the men, a Chinese, was identified by us as Wong Wei Yan. The other, a European, is a friend of Wong's named Robert Duncan. The Metropolitan Police have since discovered that Wong Wei Yan was involved with Alison Blair. The late half-sister of Roberet Duncan."

"Deceased?" inquired Inspector Choi.

"Yes, she was killed in a car accident. Just before the wedding with Wong."

"Then the two men already knew each other?"

"That is to be assumed. At least the two men have known each other since university. There, their friendship seemed to deepen. - On 24 June this year, Tung was sent pictures of his daughter to the office. When the Flying Squad arrived at the girl's school, Mui had already been kidnapped. - It was not until two days later, on 26 June, that the kidnappers came forward. Tung Ming Wah had to return to Hong Kong. It is suspected that this was an act of revenge by Wong Wei Yan.

"We have checked all incoming flights in Hong Kong. We know from the Hong Kong customs authorities that Robert Duncan and Wong Wei Yan entered Hong Kong on 26 June. There is no trace of ten-year-old Mui. We suspect that she was brought to

Asia via another route and then smuggled into Hong Kong. We have not yet been able to prove this. The kidnappers had sent messages to Tung telling him where to go to get the next message. At Madame Tussauds, they played him a mobile phone. On the display was a picture of his daughter Mui, who does not seem to be in good health. Since then, Tung has been receiving text messages with instructions from the kidnappers. Always from different numbers, each time from a different place. The kidnappers are very careful. There is no area to probe.

"Fifty-eight kilograms of cocaine were demanded in exchange for Mui. - Tonight, on the Avenue of the Stars, during the laser show, the delivery of a cocaine sample took place. So much for our case.

"Now we come to the point that will be interesting for you, Inspector. Tung organised a list of all the Yi Wong's properties on his own yesterday. He used a contact he already knew through his investigation of the Yi Wong at the time. ..."

Now Choi took the floor.

"Johnny Lee. Wong must have found out somehow. Because when we arrived at Johnny Lee's house this afternoon, he had been made an example of. Hands, feet and head had been cut off and laid beside his body. I could already confirm that Johnny Lee was a member of the Yi Wong. So in that case, we must also focus on the Yi Wong."

"That's right. Maybe we can give you some more information: Tung's best friend and former partner, Chow Nie Wen, is Wong's half-brother. Since we have Chow checked out, we know that he had spoken to

Wong on the phone at noon today. Chow seems to be involved in this. However, Chow does not seem to be sympathetic to Wong. Nor does Chow seem to know where Mui is."

"Couldn't this be a set-up by those two? They must figure that at least Chow will be checked."

"Anything is possible. Also that he really doesn't know much more than we do. Tung continues to stand by his friend. So we have to be careful what we reveal in front of Tung. - On the other hand, there was a Chop team at Chow's flat this afternoon. Fortunately, Chow had not been in the flat. But since that afternoon, he has disappeared. We can't locate him. So it may be that he stepped on someone's toes."

"You mean his half-brother tried to have him killed?"

"I don't know who sent them. But Chow definitely made enemies. Of course, no one in the house saw or heard anything. So we don't have any descriptions of people."

Choi took notes. He kept writing the name "Tung" on the sheet.

"Is something wrong?" asked Cheung.

"On 2 July 1998, wasn't his car also blown up by a car bomb, killing his wife?" asked Choi.

Mei Ling looked at him questioningly. He knew him?

"That's correct," Cheung confirmed.

Choi nodded.

"I had worked on the case at the time. I had spoken to his superior several times. I didn't have much to do with Tung. Couldn't because he disappeared pretty soon. We also suspected the Yi Wong behind the attack, but we couldn't prove it. When we tried to arrest the manufacturer of the bomb, a freelance craftsman, his garage blew up in our faces. After that, we couldn't find a clue to the last person who had commissioned the bomb. - Poor guy, Tung. First his wife and now his daughter.

"But the daughter is still alive, at least we hope so."

"Where is Tung now?" asked Mei Ling.

"In his hotel room. After the escapades in the afternoon, we grounded him. Two colleagues sit outside his door and make sure he doesn't leave."

"Can you please describe him to me briefly, I can't remember exactly?" inquired Choi.

"But yes: one metre seventy-five tall, very slim, short hair, now greying, beard. Striking facial features, slightly longer nose, piercing gaze, very focused. Sometimes too pro-active."

"Quite idiosyncratic and penetrating in parts?"

"I thought you hardly had anything to do with him." teased Inspector Cheung.

The team laughed. The old story about the improperly borrowed police car and a hair-raising chase that ended in a pile-up was still circulating through the Hong Kong Police Force. This incident remained forever linked to Tung and Chow's names. In the meetings with Tung, they had then witnessed first-hand that he did not give in so easily and tried to get his way.

At that moment, Inspector Cheung's mobile phone

rang.

"Hello!"

Cheung listened with a tense expression.

"You've got to be kidding me!" shouted Inspector Cheung out of a sudden, slapping the table with the flat of his hand.

The whole crew was startled and looked at him questioningly.

"There are two of you posted outside the room. How can he get away from you?"

A blush of anger rose in Inspector Cheung's face. He listened incredulously to the further explanations.

"You come to the station immediately. And your colleague will wait in the hotel room until Tung returns!" Inspector Cheung ordered and pushed the call away.

He threw the phone on the table and took a deep breath.

"Tung tricked my people. Tricked them into the bathroom, apologised, then knocked them out, locked them in the bathroom and left the hotel room."

He rubbed his chin.

"That's all I need, a mad father now rushing around Hong Kong looking for his daughter. Damn it! Now we have to find Tung too, before he does something crazy."

His mother had always wished that Cheung would become a cook. At the moment, he wished for it himself. He felt like he was in a madhouse.

Inspector Choi had a hard time not laughing out

loud. At least that couldn't happen to him in the homicide department. At least the corpses stayed put. Even though he realised how foolish Tung's behaviour was, he was somehow impressed by this man. He only hoped that Tung did not make a mistake. Inspector Choi looked around. They all hoped so.

"I hope he is still sensible enough. After all, he is a policeman," said Inspector Choi.

"I'm afraid at the moment he's too much of a father to be a policeman," Inspector Cheung replied.

"As soon as we have something that might help you, we'll be in touch. And we'll keep our eyes open about Tung." Inspector Choi assured.

"Thank you very much! We'll keep in touch."

"Of course."

Inspector Choi and Mei Ling left the room. They had received some information.

Meanwhile, Inspector Cheung and his team's meeting continued.

"After having played so badly with Tung's informant, it should now be clear to everyone that the kidnappers will stop at nothing.

"The delivery of the cocaine sample this evening went according to plan. In the newspaper there was again a note with a number. This time it was 48. So this is actually a countdown. The delivery of the cocaine will probably take place on 2 July around 8 p.m.. - Lee, what's the status on getting the cocaine ready for the handover? Have we got the clearance?"

"Only needs to be signed by the Superintendent.

He was not available today. I'll go and see him again tomorrow. Shouldn't be a problem though. Apart from getting our heads ripped off if we lose the cocaine," Officer Lee replied.

At the last remark, some team members rolled their eyes. Everyone was aware of the trouble the loss of the cocaine from the evidence room would cause. But Inspector Cheung immediately dismissed it.

"We are aware of that, Lee. But until we have more specific information about the nature, location and timing of the handover, we can't plan a backup. Get the authorisation so that we have everything ready, provided the further rules of the game are clarified."

"Will do."

"If we find Mui first, we won't need the cocaine," a colleague interjected with a grin.

"Let's hope so! So let's turn to the theory that Mui is probably being held in the flat at 425 Queens Road West. The suspicion has since been strengthened. Tung received a message sent to the hotel around noon, consisting of a photograph of the house. A window was circled in the photo. And that window just happens to belong to the Yi Wong's flat."

With these words, Inspector Cheung placed the photograph on the blueprint of the building, which was already on the table.

"Who would send us this information?" asked Mary.

"Maybe the same person who sent Tung the pictures of his daughter to the office?" thought Keung aloud.

"So we have someone on our side? Could that possibly have been Chow?"

Keung shook his head.

"If he was really on Tung's side, he would have freed Mui himself by now. No, I don't think so."

"Neither do I," Inspector Cheung joined in the deliberations. "Still, it could just as easily be part of the cat-and-mouse game and they just want to wear him down even more. Or send us on a false trail." Inspector Cheung indicated. "Keung, what did your observations of the building reveal?"

"Someone is moving there. It seems to be a flying change. All day long there are two furniture transporters in front of the house. Carpets, cupboards, boards and boxes are constantly being loaded or unloaded." Keung remarked.

"Were you able to get anything from the property manager?"

"Not really. He's in hospital with a broken leg."

"So how do we proceed? We should definitely keep an eye on the Englishman. Ming and Sam, you'll shadow him. I want to know what he's doing and who he's meeting. Here's the address of the hotel. Go there and then stay on his tail."

"What do we do with Tung?"

"I'll have someone look for him. There's nothing else we can do for him at the moment."

"Before handing over the cocaine sample, had he at least said what had happened in the afternoon?"

"No. But he did something, I bet. I just don't know what. For the moment, though, that doesn't get us anywhere. Let's concentrate on the mission tomorrow morning..."

Inspector Cheung picked up one of the blueprints and pinned it to the noticeboard behind him for the whole team to see.

30 June 2005, 23:45, Hong Kong Island, Queens Road West

Mei Ling was waiting for Inspector Choi in front of the house. Two young policemen were standing with her. Inspector Choi got out of the car and stifled a yawn. She held out a paper cup to him.

"Coffee." she said shortly.

Inspector Choi gratefully accepted the cup.

"Oh, we're supposed to wear these too," Mei Ling added, handing him another simple breathing mask. "Tear gas was used there and it hasn't completely dissipated yet."

Inspector Choi took the mask and looked questioningly at Mei Ling. They had already had a long day. They had only separated about an hour ago and now Mei Ling was standing in front of him again, fresh and alert, and had gotten both of them coffee.

"Anything wrong?"

"Why are you still so full of energy? You were tired earlier, too, weren't you?" he wanted to know.

They went into the building.

"All I have to do is sit down in a comfortable chair, sleep for ten to fifteen minutes and then I'm back in top form."

"Ten to fifteen minutes?" he asked incredulously.

"Yes."

The young policeman who led them to the flat turned around.

"Powersleeping?" he asked Mei Ling.

"Yes, exactly. Do you do that too?"

"I read about it in a magazine. Does it really work? I try it all the time, but I can't fall asleep that quickly. And I usually end up sleeping longer and being all the more tired afterwards," the policeman admitted.

"Oh, you have to be careful that they don't lie completely flat. Then it's also easier to get your head free of everything," Mei Ling encouraged him.

"Can you tell us anything about the situation?" asked Inspector Choi, turning the topic back to the crime scene.

"Four men were shot. Each victim has at least five bullet wounds, the doctor said. In an adjoining room there is only a mattress on the floor." the policeman informed them.

"Where is the room?" asked Inspector Choi.

The young police officer led them both through the living room where the four men who had been shot had just been cleared for removal by the coroner.

"Has this room been cleared by forensics yet?" asked Inspector Choi.

"Photographs and the first rough forensics have already been done. The detailed work is still ongoing."

"Call me someone from forensics, please."

Inspector Choi walked towards the mattress lying on the floor in the far corner. Mei Ling followed him tensely. An employee from the Identification Bureau came in.

"How can I help?"

"Have you photographed the cardigan yet?"

"Yes, we have already photographed everything. But nothing else has been touched yet."

"Can I have a closer look at that cardigan?"

"I think so. Wait, I'll get you some disposable gloves."

"Thank you."

When Inspector Choi had put on the gloves, he pulled at the tip of a cardigan that was peeking out from under the rumpled bed.

"This is a child's cardigan?" cried Mei Ling in horror.

Inspector Choi turned to her and then looked back at the cardigan he was still holding up.

"I guess I'd better call Inspector Cheung."

The colleague from forensics and the young policeman who had stayed with them were also staring at the cardigan.

"Inspector, I'm in front of the door for a moment," Mei Ling murmured softly and walked out of the room.

Inspector Choi took out his mobile phone and dialled Inspector Cheung's number. How good that he had already saved the number.

'What's going on here?' mused Inspector Choi as he waited for a connection. A man's extremities had been cut off in the morning and placed next to his body. And now the four men who had been shot. Was there a connection between these two murders? All this seemed to be connected to the abducted Tung Ai

Mui. What had happened to her now? Was she still alive?

Inspector Choi put the cardigan into the plastic bag that the forensics colleague was holding out for him.

"I want the jacket to come to the lab immediately and be examined."

"You can count on it. But if we find something so that a DNA analysis can be carried out, it will take at least 14 hours," the colleague from the Identification Bureau explained to Inspector Choi.

"All right. But I want the report right away then."

Inspector Choi left the room. He went in search of the bathroom, where he suspected Mei Ling was. But he found her already in the hallway. Leaning against a wall and as white as a sheet. There was not much left of the lively, bright young woman who had been waiting for him outside the house earlier.

"Sorry."

"For what?"

"Because I had to get out."

"Actually, I expected this reaction from you already this morning."

"I was still able to distract myself then. - Have you reached Inspector Cheung?"

"Yes. He'll be over in a minute."

"Hopefully the girl is still alive."

"We all hope so."

Mei Ling had to think of her little sister. Who was Mui's age. How could anyone do such a thing to a child?

"Come on, go home, Mei Ling. I'll sort some things out and wait for Cheung."

Without waiting for an answer, he put his arm around her slender shoulders and directed her out of the flat.

It was good for Inspector Choi to get to know Mei Ling from the human side. She was not as hard-boiled as she always seemed.

1 July 2005, 09:00, Hong Kong Island, HKPF Crime Wing HK Island Regional Headquarters

Cheung's investigation team was restless. They had heard about the murders in the flat when Cheung had cancelled the mission to free Mui. But none of them knew the details. Just then, Inspector Cheung, Inspector Choi and Mei Ling entered the briefing room. Choi and Cheung had dark circles under their eyes. They seemed to have been awake all night discussing the cases and looking for answers.

"Good morning, everyone. You already know Inspector Choi and Mei Ling. Unfortunately, something has come up that requires another joint briefing. Inspector, you have the floor." With these words, Inspector Cheung sat down at the briefing table with his team. Mei Ling sat down next to him while Inspector Choi began to summarise the latest events.

"As you have already learned, there was a small massacre yesterday in the flat where you suspected little Tung Ai Mui to be. Here are a few of the shots that the forensics team took."

"We found four men shot in the living room. In an adjoining room, a mattress was lying on the floor and a cardigan was peeking out from under the bedclothes. When we pulled it out, we saw that it was a child's cardigan. Probably part of a school uniform. Whether this is a school uniform from Tung Ai Mui's school is being checked by the Met in London right now."

He put the copies of all the reports received and

written so far regarding the body findings of the previous day on the table.

"Here are copies of all the reports we currently have on the two murder cases. Unfortunately, the last report from the coroner's office is still pending. The DNA pattern of Mui could already be sent to us by the Met due to hair in her brush. So we will then be able to quickly determine if it is the same DNA pattern. But we won't know that until later this afternoon."

Inspector Cheung looked around. He could almost hear their fears.

"Do you think something happened to Ai Mui?"

"I don't know."

He looked at the tense faces of the team. They had planned the access and the possible rescue of Mui in detail. With this turn of events, they now had to start the search all over again. And Mui's life was probably in even greater danger.

"No traces of blood were found in the bed or in the room. Therefore, we hope that Tung Ai Mui did not come to any harm."

A quiet sigh of relief could be heard.

"So we know that Tung Ai Mui was most likely held in this flat. But we don't know where she is now or who did the massacre. None of the neighbours claim to have heard anything. No one has seen the girl."

"What about the movers." Keung asked.

"None of the neighbours had paid attention to them. We couldn't get any concrete descriptions that would have sufficed for phantom pictures. Otherwise we would have to lock up the whole of Hong Kong in prison."

"I have pictures." said Keung.

"Excuse me?" Everyone looked at Keung with astonished looks.

"I have pictures. Of all the people who entered or left the building yesterday."

"Why didn't you say that yesterday?" Inspector Cheung asked.

"Because yesterday they were just movers and today they are potential murderers and kidnappers - or witnesses."

"Why did you take their pictures?" asked Mary.

"I wanted to try out the new mobile phone that I had bought the night before last. And since I had to watch the house and I was bored, I just took pictures of the movers."

Keung could not hide a certain pride in his voice, although he tried to appear quite nonchalant.

That was truly a lucky coincidence. Maybe it was a way to get on a new track.

"Does Tung Ming Wah perhaps know something? Does he have a hunch? Or haven't you told him yet?" Mei Ling turned to Inspector Cheung.

"I'm afraid I can't answer that. He hasn't shown up since last night," Inspector Cheung remarked.

"What about Chow?"

"Also untraceable. – Every police officer in Hong Kong is looking for them, but at the moment we don't know where they are. Calls and messages are not being answered, phones are switched off. We can't locate them, we can't contact them, nothing."

"Where do we go from here?" asked Keung.

"You deliver your pictures to the Identification Bureau. Let them try to find out the names of the men."

Then he turned to Inspector Choi.

"I'm sorry we can't help you at the moment. As soon as we have the pictures and names of the removal men, we will pass them on to you. Would you please inform me as soon as you have news from England?"

"Of course."

Inspector Choi and Mei Ling got up and left the room.

"Mary, how's the Englishman's tail?"

"At about 10 p.m. he was taken to the hotel by Wong Wei Yan. He entered the hotel immediately. Wong Wei Yan's car drove away. Thirty minutes later he left the hotel again. He took a taxi to Wan Chai and went to a restaurant there."

"Do they know why? Did he eat there?"

"Ming had followed him into the restaurant, but the Englishman was nowhere to be seen. It should be of interest, however, that the restaurant is owned by none other than Dai Lou Chan."

A low murmur went through the room.

"Half an hour later, the Englishman came out again, got into a taxi and drove to the hotel. He then stayed there overnight. This morning, Sam was told that the Englishman had already checked out and was flying back to London early this afternoon."

"Good. Please pass this information on to the Met team. Then they can follow his heels when he gets back there."

"I have already arranged that."

"Good, let's see if there's anything else interesting to hear from the Englishman. Mary, have Sam and Ming come back here when he made it through Security. - Keung, you take care of the pictures you took and the list of names. - Lee, get in touch with the Superintendent. I don't think we'll need the cocaine anymore, but I want it handy in case we do. - All right, folks, I think we have some work left on the tables. The next meeting is at noon."

With that, Inspector Cheung collected the documents scattered on the table and left the room.

1 July 2005, 10:09 a.m., Hong Kong Island, HKPF Crime Wing HK Island Regional Headquarters

Inspector Cheung entered the visiting room and stood wide-legged in front of Wah with his arms folded in front of his chest. There sat Tung Ming Wah calmly on the sofa, as if nothing had ever happened. Inspector Cheung took a deep breath.

"The prodigal son is back. How nice!" he greeted Wah cynically.

Wah only nodded with a faint smile, but remained silent.

"Come with me." the Inspector urged Wah.

Wah rose and followed the Inspector into his office. Followed by many pairs of eyes.

"Where were you?" asked Inspector Cheung after he sat down behind his desk.

"I had to sort something out."

"Oh well, that was probably also much more important than letting us do our work in peace and cooperate."

"It was important."

"More important than your daughter's life and the successful liberation of your daughter?"

Inspector Cheung was seething with anger. That Wah still remained so calm only made him angrier.

"I went to see Mui and had to make sure she was OK," Wah said quietly.

"WHAT?"

"Mui is safe."

Inspector Cheung went to the office door.

"Mary, Keung, in my office now!" he yelled and returned to his seat.

Mary and Keung, who had already seen Wah when he entered, came in curiously. Inspector Cheung took a dictaphone out of the desk drawer and switched it on.

"So, Tung, now there are more witnesses here. Would you please repeat your last sentence?!"

"Mui is safe."

Inspector Cheung saw the looks on Mary's and Keung's faces. He raised his eyebrows and nodded at the two.

"Mui is safe. Did you hear that?"

Both nodded. Inspector Cheung stood up.

"I'm going out for a few minutes. And you two make sure he doesn't leave again. He must not leave the room. If necessary, shoot him! "

With these words, Inspector Cheung left the office. He had to get himself under control again. He was aware that his behaviour was completely exaggerated, but at the moment it was the only thing that kept him from punching Tung with rage. He went into the washroom and ran ice-cold water over his wrists and hands and submerged his face under water.

Ten minutes later, Inspector Cheung entered his office again. Tung, Mary and Keung were still there. And as he entered, he heard Tung say "...Mui is relatively well." But when Wah saw Inspector

Cheung, he fell silent again.

"Okay, now I would like to know from the beginning what happened yesterday, please."

"Yesterday at noon I just had to find out if I could still trust Nie Wen. I had seen that he had left his flat and went over to his flat. He's a creature of habit, so I was able to gain access to his flat relatively easily. Inside the flat, I looked for clues."

"What kind of clues?" asked Inspector Cheung.

"Any. I had checked whether he really received money from the Yi Wong. But I just didn't know to what extent he might have been involved in the kidnapping after all."

"Did you find what you were looking for?"

"Yes. When I was looking through his folders, a blueprint fell into my hands, hidden behind the folders. It was the blueprint of a building."

"About the Yi Wong flat where we thought Mui was?"

"Yes."

"And then?"

"Then he called me to get out of his flat."

"Which you then did, depositing yourself à la Jackie Chan over the gutter."

Wah cleared his throat.

"What happened next?"

"I left the building and first had to sort out my thoughts."

"Why didn't you come to us?"

"Two corners down, Nie Wen approached me."

"That still doesn't explain why you didn't come to us. In fact, all you had to do was call and we would have come or at least had you picked up."

"There was an altercation with Nie Wen."

"Did he beat you up like that?"

"We both look like this."

"I hope you never want to make friends with me," Inspector Cheung said mockingly.

Mary and Keung had to smile.

"Why didn't he come to us?"

"Would you have believed him? You had him under surveillance all along anyway."

"You know the procedure. You had already failed to comply in England, so we had to take precautions."

Wah snorted briefly. Although he knew exactly that Inspector Cheung was right.

"He could have at least tried. After all, he was with the Hong Kong Police Force long enough and had excellent evaluations and commendations for his service here. This action certainly does not strengthen confidence in his loyalty to you or to us."

"Just before I was about to strike again, he shouted 'She's there!'" Wah continued. "Until now, it had only ever been a suspicion that she might be there. But all of a sudden it was confirmed."

"You should have contacted us from that moment at the latest."

"From that moment on, I had only one thought: I wanted Mui! And I wanted it now!"

Inspector Cheung slapped the desk top with the flat of his hand and jumped up out of his chair.

"You knew we had an operation planned for this morning!"

His voice almost rolled over.

"I wanted her back *right away*, Inspector," Wah replied calmly.

"Do you think we are scouts who have nothing else to do but play cops and robbers every day?"

"No." Wah replies, now slightly ashamed.

"Good, because neither do we! We've been dealing with abductions for years. And *you* are definitely not the first father whose daughter has been kidnapped. Definitely not."

"I know." said Wah.

Inspector Cheung forced himself to sit quietly in his chair again.

"Okay, you fight with Chow, he confirms to you that Mui is indeed in the flat and you already have a well thought out plan in your head? You must be a mastermind!"

"No, I'm not. - Nie Wen informed me about his plan."

"I hope you're not proud of it too."

"No, I'm not. - But I'm glad I could finally sleep last night, hold Mui in my arms and hear her breathing."

"What kind of plan was that? Go in, shoot everyone and walk out with Mui?"

Wah raised his eyebrows and looked at Inspector Cheung in surprise.

"Something like that. Except for the shooting. We are policemen, not butchers," he finally said.

"Your actions cast doubt on your being police officers, Wah. Nie Wen hasn't been one for a few years at least anyway," Inspector Cheung remarked pointedly.

But then he wanted to know how the liberation of Ai Mui was possible at all.

"We had the house watched all the time, there are even pictures of all the people who went in and out of there, but none of the pictures have you or Chow in them," said Inspector Cheung.

"We wore masks."

Inspector Cheung was not the only one who looked puzzled at that moment. This explained why a few of the men photographed could not be identified.

"Nie Wen has an acquaintance who works in the film industry. Nie Wen had already had an expensive and time-consuming make-up done that morning. That's why your men couldn't recognise him in the hotel foyer when he checked in."

"And the mask survived the beating?" inquired Mary.

"No, not quite. It had to be patched up in a makeshift way. With a little make-up, it wasn't so much noticeable from a distance. With me, it was only helped with make-up, so that the facial features no longer resembled mine. because of the swelling, it wasn't difficult."

"If you had come to us, you could have saved yourself the trouble of putting it on."

"What were those people moving there?"

"People who owed Nie Wen a favour. There was no moving. Nie Wen had already had some furniture stored on the roof, so it wasn't noticeable when people carried the same furniture in and out again and again. They had also got different coloured doors for the cupboards, so it always looked like different furniture."

"Long live IKEA." grumbled Inspector Cheung. "By the way, did you know that most of the men belong to Dai Lou Chan?"

Wah looked at Inspector Cheung in disbelief.

"The Dai Lou Chan from Wan Chai?"

"Yes. - Does Chow have any connections to Dai Lou Chan?"

Wah shook his head. Dai Lou Chan was a household name to him. And he knew how dangerous this man could become. So how was it that Nie Wen hired his people? To what extent did they owe him a favour?

But Inspector Cheung, noticing that Wah had been surprised by this news, did not want to give him time for musings. At least not at the moment.

"Go on." urged Inspector Cheung.

"We mingled with the men and went into the house. When one of the guards wanted to leave the flat, we fell upon him, went back into the flat with him and while Nie Wen held the people at gunpoint, I searched for Mui. She was fast asleep in an adjoining room. The bastards had pumped her full of sleeping pills to get some peace."

At these words, not only did his voice begin to tremble slightly, but his hands shook as well. The worries he had about her health and the pressure he had been under in the last few days were obvious. But he got himself under control again.

Inspector Cheung and Keung looked at each other silently, but their expressions betrayed that they were angry. Mary pressed her fingernails into her palms to keep the anger in check through the pain.

"I got Mui out of there and Nie Wen followed. He had set off a tear gas grenade so they were not able to follow us. We didn't go out of the house immediately, but ran up the stairs first. At the top they had been waiting with a wardrobe prepared for Mui to be taken away."

"Where is Mui now?"

"We took her to her grandparents, my wife's parents. Ai Ling's father practices traditional Chinese medicine. And who else could help her better now?"

"A hospital, perhaps? Where they could detoxify her?"

Wah just looked at Inspector Cheung in silence.

"He is a good doctor. If he realises he can't help Mui, he will take her to hospital."

"Where is Chow now?"

"He has taken Mui and the grandparents to a safe hiding place. Only when everything is over and Wong Wei Yan is arrested will Nie Wen return with them."

"You know there will be consequences for this."

"Yes."

"Chow too?"

"Yes."

Inspector Cheung nodded and exhaled loudly again. He was glad that Mui was safe, even if he did not like the approach at all. Not at all.

Inspector Cheung rose from his chair, paced around his desk, walked up to Wah and extended his hand. Wah also stood up and took the hand offered to him.

Just then, the handcuffs clicked. Wah looked questioningly at Inspector Cheung.

"Tung Ming Wah, you are hereby arrested for contravening existing laws, obstructing police work in the 'Tung Ai Mui' abduction case, assault in two cases on police officers on duty, unauthorised possession of weapons, repeated trespassing and murder in four cases."

"How long are you actually going to hold him?" Keung asked Inspector Cheung as he grinned smugly to himself.

"Until we have taken on Wong Wei Yan," he said with relish. "It will do Tung good to have some rest. And it's good for us that he can't interfere again and jeopardise the next mission."

After these words, he bit into his sandwich again.

As Inspector Cheung had taken an unknown person - namely Tung Ming Wah - out of the equation by arresting him, he invited the team for sandwiches, which they now ate during the meeting.

The kidnapping had ended prematurely, but the kidnappers were still to be brought to justice, which, however, was difficult without a hostage and thus the urgent suspicion of the crime. The only thing that could help now was the evidence found in the flat.

"Do you think Tung and Chow killed the men?" asked Officer Lee.

Inspector Cheung shook his head.

"No. He reacted with surprise when I mentioned the shooting."

"Could have been an act."

"No." Inspector Cheung defended himself. "I don't trust Tung with such a slaughter. He was serious when he said 'We are policemen, not butchers'."

"Well, he has already done one or two things that

one would deny a policeman or any clear-thinking person. With that action, they had unnecessarily put Mui's life in far greater danger than she was already in," remarked Keung, who could certainly understand Officer Lee's train of thought. If he had not been present during the conversation with Wah, he would probably have thought the same.

"Still. He had Mui. She had been drugged, but she was still alive," Mary pointed out.

"So he would have been able to do it after all if she had not lived?" Officer Lee probed further.

"We don't know that. And we don't have to guess about that. Mui is alive and presumably safe and in medical care at the moment. We have other problems to solve."

"So we still don't know where she is now?"

"No. He doesn't say a word. He doesn't want to take any chances."

"Why does he trust Chow and not us?"

"Whether he trusts Chow or not remains to be seen."

"But..." Mary was about to start when a colleague knocked on the door and entered.

"Inspector, here are the coroner's records."

With these words, he handed the envelope to Inspector Cheung and left the room again.

"Thank you."

Inspector Cheung opened the envelope, took out the documents inside and read. The team looked at him eagerly. After a few minutes, Inspector Cheung put the report on the table.

"These are the documents Inspector Choi promised us. - The cardigan was confirmed by the Met as part of the school uniform of Mui's school. There were also hair of hers found on it. In addition, there were a few other hair whose DNA could already be determined as far as possible, but no comparisons have been made yet. At the moment, it is still being checked whether these are from the murdered persons. We have to consider that she was already wearing the jacket since the abduction."

"Was there anything else new?"

"The firearm used to shoot the four men has been identified."

"Well?"

The team looked tensely at Inspector Cheung.

"Not the models Wah and Nie Wen had."

"So then there's someone else we need to focus on."

"No, who Inspector Choi has to focus on. For now, we'll stick to cornering Wong Wei Yan and having his friend followed. I still think he's the mastermind behind the kidnapping. - Mary, any news from the guys?"

"No. Not yet."

"Lee, did you get anywhere with the Superintendent?"

"All cleared and signed. Should we need the cocaine, it's ready."

"I do hope we won't need it, but it's good to be

prepared for anything. – Now let's plan our visit to Wong Wei Yan today."

With these words, he revealed the view of the blueprints of Highcliff.

1 July 2005, 13:48, Hong Kong, Lantau Island, Chek Lap Kok International Airport

"This will probably be the shortest tail in the history of the Hong Kong Police Force," Sam told Ming.

Both police officers strolled through the airport, keeping an eye on Robert Duncan, who was just leaving the check-in counter.

"That's right. Last night the order and now the Englishman is already flying off back to London. In London, the men of the Met can follow his heels."

They saw Robert go through a door secured by police officers. Behind it were only the passport and security checks, the duty-free shops and then the gates.

"Done. Let's go back to the office."

"No, wait a minute, Sam. - Let's take the opportunity for a little break. Listen, I have to go to the bathroom first. Go to Pacific Coffee and order us something. Get me one of those brownies, too. I also want to check my e-mails. So take a mouse with you and sit down at a free computer."

"Any other requests?"

"No, a brownie and a medium coffee will do. Thank you!"

Ming just left Sam in front of the small Vertu shop and went to the restroom. Sam grumbled, but then went to one of the two Pacific Coffee Shops and did as he was told.

Twenty minutes later, Ming reappeared.

"Man, what took you so long?" Sam grumbled at him.

Ming wordlessly picked up the brownie and bit into it.

"Mmmh, that feels good. Thank you," he said with his mouth full.

"You owe me 175 HKDollar."

"What, for a coffee and a brownie?"

"One hundred dollars rental fee for the mouse."

"Oh, you'll get it back anyway. - Here's seventy-five dollars."

Ming pulled his wallet out of his pocket and handed Sam the amount owed.

"Besides, I already called the office and said that the Englishman was out of range for us. - We should have contacted the department at the airport, then we could have seen him get on the plane..."

"Says who?"

"Mary."

"Next time, she can do the shadowing. When he takes off..."

That was as far as Ming got. Because Sam had grabbed his arm and was staring past Ming with wide eyes.

"What is it?"

Ming turned around as he swallowed the last bite. And then he saw it too. Or rather 'him'.

Not forty metres away from them, Robert Duncan ran across one of the connecting bridges to the exit of the airport.

He didn't just walk, he ran.

Sam immediately terminated the internet connection and ran off.

"Hey, and the mouse?!" exclaimed Ming.

"Forget the mouse.... We have to get to the car!"

As soon as Sam and Ming were in their car and following Duncan's taxi, Ming called the office.

"Mary, the Englishman has turned up again. He just ran out of the airport and got into a taxi."

"Damn, where the hell is this guy going?" asked Ming aloud after he had finished the phone call.

"I don't know. " Sam remarked briefly, sitting behind the steering wheel and making sure not to lose sight of the taxi, which was travelling at the maximum permitted speed.

"There definitely seems to be something off, the way he was running," Sam thought out loud.

Ming nodded. What was the Englishman up to? Why hadn't he got on the plane? And why was he in such a damn hurry?

So this was not the shortest tail in the history of the Hong Kong Police Force after all.

1 July 2005, 13:53, Hong Kong Island, 41D Stubbs Road, Highcliff

Yan was surprised when Ruby told him that Kwong Wai Ming wanted to talk to him. Yan stood up to meet his fatherly friend when he entered Yan's study.

"Lou Kwong, what a surprise. To what do I owe the honour of your visit?" Yan inquired, gesturing for Kwong Wai Ming to sit down on the comfortable sofa.

Kwong Wai Ming did not answer, but simply sat down.

"May I offer you some tea?" asked Yan.

"Yes. It's easier to negotiate over tea," Kwong Wai Ming said in a low raspy voice.

Yan looked at him questioningly. What did he mean by 'negotiate'? But Yan looked up again at Ruby, who was still standing in the doorway.

"Please bring us tea, Ruby."

Ruby nodded and closed the door behind her. Yan sat down opposite Kwong Wai Ming. He briefly looked at his watch, which Kwong Wai Ming noticed.

"A date?" he asked curiously.

"Yes."

"With whom?"

"In Wan Chai." Yan evaded the question.

Yan did not want to tell him that Dai Lou Chan had invited him. Mr. Chan wanted to tell him who the black sheep in the Yi Wong was.

"That's not what I asked," Kwong Wai Ming

remarked sourly. "But I want to keep it short so you won't be late."

"Thank you."

Yan was glad not to be asked any more questions. However, he would never have expected what was coming up now in his wildest dreams.

"Where is the child?" asked Kwong Wai Ming straightforwardly.

"Who?" Yan raised his eyebrows.

"The child. Where is she?"

"What child, Lou Kwong?" asked Yan again, completely puzzled.

For the time being, Kwong Wai Ming did not reply. Ruby opened the door and entered the study with a tray to serve the tea. Only after Ruby had left the room did Kwong Wai Ming answer.

"The kid you took from the flat?"

"What are you talking about?" asked Yan.

But suddenly he knew what Kwong Wai Ming was talking about. It was as if a door had opened and Yan now saw the whole truth.

Yan remembered Dai Lou Chan's remark at the last meeting. '...It is always good to have someone who can bring people to Hong Kong relatively unnoticed'. Mr. Chan had known about the kidnapping of the child!

Suddenly, all the other pieces of the puzzle seemed to fit together in his mind's eye. For years he had tried to legalise the Yi Wong. For years he had been sabotaged again and again. He knew it was someone inside the Yi Wong, but he could never find out who was behind it.

But now, at this moment, he knew.

Yan was shocked.

All these years, Yan had not noticed that it was Lou Kwong who was trying to boycott all of Yan's ventures. How could he have been so blind? Presumably *that* was exactly the information Dai Lou Chan wanted to give him right at the meeting.

"Ah! I see you get it now." remarked Kwong Wai Ming snidely.

"You rat." said Yan stretched.

Yan jumped up from his seat, but at that moment Kwong Wai Ming was already drawing his revolver.

"Easy, boy."

"Don't call me boy! *I am* the Chairman of the Yi Wong!" said Yan angrily and threateningly. But he only received a derisive laugh.

"Chairman. Ha! Don't make me laugh. You are a nobody. You were never really the Chairman. And you never will be. Too soft. Too stupid. - I should have been Chairman. I knew everything about the syndicate. I was your father's best friend. I was his confidant. Yet, though you had disappointed him time and again, he had appointed you as his successor. What a fool!"

"Don't talk about my father like that. If he was a fool, it was because he thought you were his best friend!" Yan retorted angrily.

"As if. I was the only one who could make sure your father wasn't abandoned. It was ME who held the syndicate together. Or do you think your father was only so neglectful towards you. Oh, no. He even allowed your brother what he always denied you: a life outside the syndicate. Worse than that. He was even allowed to join the police. Surprised? - Yeah, I can see it in your face. You didn't know. Did you? Not even guessed?"

Kwong Wai Ming fell into a derisive laugh again, this time followed by the rattling cough. Nevertheless, he kept Yan at bay with his revolver.

Yan was completely overwhelmed. He had guessed that there was another child. Illegitimate. But he had never found any proof. His father had never spoken about it. His mother... No. She had her whisky, her friends whom she met over five-o-clock tea at the Peninsula Hotel to show off the latest purchases. She had retreated into her own life. Maybe she had known or sensed. But she had never said anything.

"Why are you doing this?" asked Yan quietly, sitting down again.

"Money. And power."

"How so? You were the second man in the syndicate."

Kwong Wai Ming rolled his eyes contemptuously. How he hated always being the second man.

"Yes. And you've made sure that both are a little complicated."

"Then I am not as stupid as you claim." Yan teased him.

He could see that Kwong Wai Ming would have

liked to pull the trigger.

"Where is the child?"

"What child?"

"The policeman's daughter."

"So you kidnapped the child and brought her to Hong Kong."

"Yes, I did."

"Why?"

"Why? Because of money, of course! And revenge."

Yan could still understand revenge as a response. For decades, Lou Kwong had been his father's right-hand man. The fact that Yan was named by his father in his will as the new Chairman must have been a blow to Lou Kwong.

But money?

Yan was beginning to feel like a silly boy. 'Of course,' he scolded himself, 'he's blackmailing the father.' Unfortunately, however, the bastard was holding a gun at him.

"How much?"

"Fifty-eight kilograms of cocaine."

Yan whistled through his teeth. That was a fortune.

"And then you just let the child be snatched from under your nose?" asked Yan with a playfully incredulous look.

He couldn't help himself and now drilled a little into the wound Kwong Wai Ming had just presented.

"Where is she?" the latter asked angrily.

Yan began to grin all over his face, pronouncing each word emphatically one by one.

"I-don't-know."

"You'll lose that stupid grin of yours, boy." hissed Kwong Wai Ming, raising his revolver as the door of the study was suddenly yanked open.

Robert stood in the doorway holding a pistol.

"Put the gun down, Kwong." he shouted.

"I don't think so." remarked Kwong Wai Ming calmly.

And already Robert felt a powerful blow on the back of his head. It went black before his eyes, he fell to his knees, the pistol slipped from his hand.

"Ruby, NO!" cried Yan in horror. "What have you done?"

Kwong Wai Ming laughed.

"What a woman must do to protect her lover," Kwong Wai Ming said calmly.

Yan's eyes snapped open. Mistress? Of Kwong Wai Ming?

Ruby lowered her eyes and turned around without a word. Yan had been like a child of her own to her. But she had fallen for Kwong since her youth. She had always hoped never to come between the two. Because she knew she would never abandon Kwong.

1 July 2005, 2:23 p.m., Hong Kong Island, 41D Stubbs Road, Highcliff

The lift stopped on the 67th floor and the doors opened. Cautiously, Ming and Sam peered outside. No one was to be seen in the corridor. Good. They went to the right. There was the door. Above the doorbell was the name: Wong Wei Yan.

Ming was about to press the bell button when Sam grabbed him by the arm.

"Are you crazy?" asked Sam in a whisper.

"Why? That's why we're here, isn't it?" Ming also replied in a whisper.

"No. We have taken up the pursuit. We are here. And now we wait until the others are here."

"Shall we knock and see what happens?"

"No. We shan't. No way," Sam hissed.

As the door suddenly opened from the inside, there was no need for further discussion. Because now Ruby stood in front of them and flinched in fright. Behind her stood Kwong Wai Ming, who pressed the revolver against Yan's back.

Ming was the first to find the language again.

"Good afternoon, madam. We are from the police and would like to talk to Wong Wei Yan."

With these words he held up his police ID card.

Sam could not believe his ears.

Kwong Wai Ming panicked. He jumped to the side, jerked up his hand with the revolver and aimed at Ming.

"No!" Ruby shouted and wanted to get to safety.

Instead, she ran into the bullet that Kwong Wai Ming had just fired. The bullet hit Ruby in the chest. Ruby fell into Ming's arms with a low yelp, knocking him off balance and throwing him backwards to the ground.

Sam jumped to the side and drew his pistol. He pressed himself against the wall so that he was out of Kwong Wai Ming's firing range.

Yan tried to knock the gun out of Kwong Wai Ming's hand, but he got out of reach with a leap that was quite nimble for a man his age and shot at Yan. Yan cried out in pain and grabbed his upper right arm. The impact of the bullet jolted him to the ground, causing him to hit his head against a piece of furniture and pass out.

Kwong Wai Ming tried to slam the door, but Ruby's legs were in the way. So he hid behind the door, facing Ming and the dead Ruby.

"Put your gun down. Now!" shouted Sam.

Secretly hoping that the requested support would soon be there.

"No." replied Kwong, who had by now regained his composure. "The only one who will put down his gun here and throw it down the hall is you, young man."

"Sir, once again I demand that you lay down your weapon immediately and surrender!"

"Do what *I* say or your colleague dies."

Ming had tried to free himself from Ruby's body, but then he saw that Kwong Wai Ming had pointed the gun at him and paused lying on the ground.

Sam rubbed his face with his free hand. Beads of sweat came to his forehead. He had never been in such a situation. What now? Would the old man actually shoot Ming? Probably. He had already shot the woman and Wong Wei Yan. Where the hell were the others? And where was the Englishman?

"You should listen to me." said Kwong Wai Ming again and fired a shot at Ming.

The bullet hit Ming in the shoulder unprotected by Ruby's body. Ming cried out.

"Stop it!" shouted Sam.

He secured his pistol and threw it down the corridor over Ming and the dead Ruby.

"It's a misery with young people nowadays. They never do what they are asked to do. And then you wonder when you have to bear the consequences." remarked Kwong Wai Ming condescendingly. "Now go slowly to your colleague so I can see you."

Sam closed his eyes for a split second. Where were the others? He stood up and walked over to Ming with his hands up.

He did not want to provoke Kwong Wai Ming with a careless movement.

"That's a good boy." remarked Kwong Wai Ming.

"Stop talking to us like we are ill-bred children. What is this all about. Where do you get off shooting Wong Wei Yan?"

A contemptuous laugh followed.

"It's not a loss. He was never a real Chairman!" Kwong Wai Ming shouted bitterly.

"Why are you so angry with him?"

"Because he's a failure. Everything his father and I built up, he wanted to undo."

"In what way?" Sam inquired.

Somehow he had the feeling that Kwong Wai Ming finally wanted to show who he was. And the more information they got, the sooner they could solve the case.

"He never wanted anything to do with his father's business. Brought the Yi Wong into 'clean waters' as he called it. To the others and me, he wanted to destroy our income."

"Of course you couldn't let that happen."

"Of course not," confirmed Kwong Wai Ming. "We joined forces and carried on under the table."

"And he didn't notice?"

"No. He was so blind. For years we were able to present him with manipulated ledgers."

"But at some point he did notice?"

"Yes, he suddenly seemed suspicious. Since I was his father's best friend and confidant, he turned to me for advice. The silly boy." remarked Kwong Wai Ming dismissively. "To me, of all people!"

Again he let out his raucous laugh, this time ending in a cough. Sam wanted to jump towards him, but despite the coughing, Kwong Wai Ming kept the gun pointed at him and gestured for him to step back. Sam obeyed.

"But why did you go to Wong Wei Yan today?"

Sam tried to stall for time. The others should be

arriving soon.

"Because he got in my way again."

"How so?"

"You think you're a clever boy, don't you? Don't you? You think you can interrogate me now and blame it on me later. But don't worry, neither you nor your partner will ever be able to pass on what I say."

After a short pause, Kwong Wai Ming continued.

"He actually seemed to suspect something. And I had set it up so well. I started spreading rumours. In England. Which also reached Hong Kong. I had set it up well. The wrath of the competition was about to hit him. But somehow he had managed to get them on his side."

"You mean you denounced him to Dai Lou Chan?"

"I framed it much more subtly and intelligently than you just put it. But the result is right."

"Did you then also give the order to kill the informant in London?"

"No, someone else has taken over. I wouldn't want to be in that person's shoes." Kwong Wai Ming remarked, chuckling. But he became serious again.

"I had to be careful. At the risk of my first plan not working, I arranged for another plot to break his neck."

"Are you saying you kidnapped the child and made it look like Wong Wei Yan did it?"

Kwong Wai Ming raised his eyebrows appreciatively.

"Exactly."

"But someone got in your way and you failed again," Sam remarked.

Kwong Wai Ming got angry and wanted to say something back, but he didn't get the chance. A shot was fired in the flat. Kwong Wai Ming pulled the trigger as he fell to the side, hit by a bullet. Simultaneously the bullet from Kwong Wai Ming's revolver narrowly missed Sam's head.

At that moment, one of the doors to the stairwell opened and some policemen, dressed in helmets and protective waistcoats, rushed into the hallway. They put on their machine guns and probed the situation. They aimed at Sam, at whose feet lay Ming and the dead Ruby.

"We're police!" shouted Sam. "There's someone else in the flat who just shot Kwong Wai Ming. There are probably two injured and two dead."

The policemen nodded at him and now concentrated on the flat.

"Don't shoot!" shouted Robert Duncan in Cantonese. "I'm coming out slowly!"

The policemen were preparing for an exchange of fire. Sam was gestured with a hand sign to move to safety. He sat down against the wall of the corridor that bordered Wong Wei Yan's flat.

At first they could only see one of Robert's hands with the revolver held upside down. He held up the other hand and moved slowly forward.

"I'm putting my gun down now," he said.

Seven policemen in full gear held their submachine guns at him. Very slowly, he got down on his knees and put the gun on the ground. Slowly he straightened up again. Now holding both hands in the air.

"Is there anyone else in the flat?" one of the policemen called out.

"As far as I know, only Wong Wei Yan. He was shot at. I don't know if he's still alive," Sam replied.

"No, there's no one else in there but him," Robert added.

The policemen told him to step away from the door. He took a big step over Ming and Ruby, who were still on the floor. Two policemen pulled him to the ground and handcuffed him while the others made a raid on the flat and secured the situation.

2 July 2005, 04:37, Police Station, Sutton, Surrey, GB

A policeman closed the door behind Inspector Field after he had entered the interrogation room. Paul Leary, who was sitting huddled in the chair anyway, flinched and looked around like a frightened animal. Inspector Field exhaled loudly, put the mug of coffee on the table and sat down. He was tired.

"Who... who are you?" asked Paul Leary in his quiet beeping voice.

"My name is Simon Field. I'm an inspector with the homicide squad. And who are you?"

"Paul. Paul Leary."

Inspector Field wrote the name on a pad.

"Would you like a coffee, Mr Leary?"

Paul Leary fussed, trying to stifle a laugh. The whole scrawny body of the young man, who already looked far too old from drug use, twitched.

"Why are you laughing?"

"Because you call me mister. Nobody calls me Mr Leary. I'm Paul."

"You are a human being. Therefore, I treat you with respect. - Would you like a coffee, Mr Leary?"

The inspector's calm voice made Paul Leary relax a little.

"Yes, please. With lots of sugar."

The Inspector stood up and opened the door.

"A coffee with lots of sugar for Mr Leary, please."

"Yes, sir."

Inspector Field closed the door and took his seat again.

"Are you responsible for the murder of the fat Chinese?" asked Paul Leary.

"I am investigating the case. What is so urgent that you absolutely have to talk to *me*?"

"I want to make a confession."

Inspector Field took a sip of coffee.

"In that case, I would like to make a video recording during our meeting. Do you agree to this?"

"A video recording?"

"Yes, so that I don't have to take notes. We can then use the recording in court. Would that be all right with you?"

"Can you just see me there or can you hear me?"

"There is a microphone on the table, you see, this little thing. So there will be picture and sound recording. Do you consent?"

Paul Leary looked at the microphone and the camera.

"Yes."

"Thank you."

Inspector Field pressed the button. A red light went on at the surveillance camera.

"And now please start with what you want to tell me."

"Actually, my buddy and I wanted to come here together. But he didn't dare come out."

"Why not?"

"Well, you hear the Chinese are so mad at us. Because of the murder of the fat man. There's even a price on our head. That's why he doesn't dare come out."

"But you dare to come out."

"Well, nothing can happen to me with the police, can it?"

"What's your buddy's name?"

"Pete Jacobs."

"When was it that Pete and you killed the Chinese?"

With these words, Inspector Field opened his workbook.

"Er, you must know that." Paul Leary was surprised.

"Mr Leary, I'd first like to find out whether I was dragged out of bed at four o'clock in the morning on a Saturday for nothing, or whether you're telling the truth. So, when did you kill the Chinese?"

"Well, it was that Thursday a week ago."

"Date?"

"What's the date today?"

Inspector Field looked at his watch. "2 July 2005."

Paul Leary counted back to the date with the help of his fingers.

"23 June."

Inspector Field nodded. The door opened, the policeman brought the cup of coffee and placed it in front of Paul Leary.

"Thank you, officer," he beeped meekly.

When the policeman had left the room again, Paul Leary asked cautiously.

"Is there anything in there?"

"I thought you wanted your coffee with lots of sugar."

"No, I mean, a truth serum or something?"

"No, why would there be anything like that in it?"

"Isn't that what the Police does?"

"No. You are misinformed. We do not work with truth serums or anything like that."

Paul Leary stirred around in the cup, lost in thought.

"Please tell me what happened that night," Inspector Field interrupted the silence.

"So, we needed money again to buy drugs."

"Pete and you?"

"Exactly."

"What kind of drugs?"

"Heroin."

"Hmm. - Go on."

"Well, we really needed money. Pete was already in a bad way. He was irritable. And as we're walking down the street, we see this fat Chinese guy."

"Had you seen him before?"

"No. First time... I think."

Paul Leary took a sip of coffee, then shook his head again.

"So we see this fat Chinese guy and we think to ourselves, he must have money. He's about to get into his Mercedes. People like that have money. So we went there."

"Didn't anyone see you?"

"No, it was late night after all."

"What time?"

"I don't know. But the pubs were already closed. - So we went. Pete leaned against the driver's door so that the fat man couldn't get in. He started to swear. But Pete just held the knife out to him."

"And what did you do?"

"I stood behind the fat man so he couldn't disappear."

"Did you also have a weapon?"

"Also just a knife. But the fat guy was probably pretty scared. Well, not at first. He threatened us. You have to imagine. We stand in front and behind him with the knives and he threatens us."

Paul Leary laughed briefly and drank some more of the coffee.

"Well, in any case, he didn't want to hand over the money."

"Then what happened?"

"I don't know exactly. But somehow he must have tried to knock the knife out of Pete's hand. Pete got out of the way and just stabbed him in the stomach. Just like that."

Paul Leary made a simple hand gesture forward.

"Well, I was startled. We just wanted to rob him.

We've done a lot of robberies. Didn't get much out of it. But no one ever got hurt. And now this. The fat man had stopped laughing and threatening."

Again he took a sip of coffee.

"Said we didn't know who we were dealing with."

"What did you do, Mr Leary?"

"Me? Jeez, I was panicking. I asked him, 'Pete, what's the big deal?' But he was just as upset as I was. While the fat man slowly but surely sank to the ground, Pete came to me. We didn't know what to do. But then Pete had an idea. 'We'll disguise this as a Chinese raid,' he said to me."

"How did he come up with that?"

"Well, he had once heard that a businessman was to be massacred in Glasgow[1] . But he survived. So Pete said that if we stabbed the fat man, people would think it was other Chinese."

"And so then you stab an already injured man just like that?"

"That wasn't us."

"But you just said that you did that with Pete, or that you were going to do that."

"Well, we did that, yes, but somehow it wasn't us. Something had gone off in our heads. We were like in a bloodlust, you know?"

"And then?"

"When we were done, we put him in his own trunk. It was a hell of a job."

---

[1] Black, D. (1991). Triad Takeover (1st ed.). Sidgwick & Jackson

"Literally."

Paul Leary nodded.

"Well. He was so fat and we hardly had any strength left, but somehow we made it."

"Hadn't he shouted?"

"No, he was so shocked after the first stab that he didn't talk much.

Inspector Field closed the file.

"What happens now?" asked Paul Leary.

"We need you to give us the address where we can find your friend. Then we also need to take his statement."

"But you're looking out for us, Inspector. Aren't you? Nothing will happen to us now, will it?"

"We do what we can, Mr Leary. It is not in the interest of the police to have witnesses or suspects killed."

He switched off the video camera and the microphone and had Paul Leary led away by a policeman. Inspector Field briefly looked at his few notes, picked up his folder and also left the room. A long day lay ahead of him.

2 July 2005, 11:10 a.m., Hong Kong Island, HKPF Crime Wing HK Island Regional Headquarters

"How is Ming?" asked Officer Lee when the team had reconvened in the briefing room for a debriefing of the case.

"He's doing quite well. He's trying his charm on the nurses and having a good time," Inspector Cheung replied with a smile on his face.

He was glad that Ming had got away well and no one else from the team had been injured.

After learning from Sam and Ming that Robert Duncan was going to Wong Wei Yan, they immediately set off. When the first shot was fired on the 67th floor, neighbours called the police, so a special unit arrived at the same time as Inspector Cheung's team. Inspector Cheung was able to give brief information that two of his people were also up there.

"Have they been able to interrogate Wong Wei Yan yet?"

"No. He's still in a coma."

"Isn't that strange?"

"An anaesthetic incident can always happen." Keung remarked.

"And what about the Englishman? Has there been any word from Robert Duncan?"

"Oh, he was able to contribute some information to the case. But only as far as he knew himself."

"So why did he return to Wong Wei Yan?"

"He received a call from Chow Nie Wen, who told him that Kwong Wai Ming was the traitor among the Yi Wong."

"How did Chow Nie Wen know that? And how did he know Robert Duncan?" asked Mary.

"Oh, you have to go back a few years," Inspector Cheung began. "When the Yi Wong raid took place in 1998, the Chairman of the Yi Wong was shot dead. You already know that. That there was a bounty on Tung Ming Wah's head and then he went to England has also been known. Shortly afterwards, it was said that Chow Nie Wen quit the police force.

"But that was not the whole truth. Kwong Wai Ming had approached him and wanted to make him a police informer. He wanted to blackmail him into revealing the identity of Chow's father. However, Chow had learned who his biological father was on his mother's deathbed. This was even during the investigation against the Yi Wong, which was led by Tung. Chow now worked even harder against the Yi Wong. But Kwong Wai Ming could not have known that.

"Chow came into agreement with his superior that he would work undercover for the police. He knew that he would then be on his own, as he was officially no longer with the police. Thus he could no longer be used as a police informer for the Yi Wong or for Kwong. But he was occasionally used in smaller transactions. So he gathered a lot of information as an insider in the last few years. However, it also became increasingly clear that the new Chairman wanted to get the Yi Wong out of illegal business and bring it into legality."

"Which, of course, Kwong and some others didn't like," Officer Lee interjected.

"True. They manipulated the books and made Wong Wei Yan believe that they were following his plan. Secretly, they continued to make a fortune from the illegal business."

"Didn't Wong Wei Yan notice?"

"It had taken him a long time to realise. At first he had also trusted Kwong and informed him about it. The latter stalled him and promised to sort it out internally. Which, of course, he didn't do. On the contrary. He spread rumours that Wong Wei Yan was planning to expand his allegedly illegal business to London. Thus, he would have stepped on the toes of the competition."

"Hence his visit to Dai Lou Chan?"

"Yes, Dai Lou Chan wanted to test him. But then he eventually realised that Wong Wei Yan wasn't behind it. Secretly, Dai Lou Chan had already suspected Kwong himself."

"What about the murder of Fat Liu?"

"That's when we got the information earlier that it was two junkies who had killed him in panic. Earlier today, one of them turned himself in to the police in Sutton. Even though everything still has to be checked, this case is probably closed."

"Why is that?"

"They had overheard that the triads had put a bounty on the killers' heads and they got scared."

"Rightly so, after some information fell into the

hands of the police through Fat Liu's life insurance policy and it had considerable repercussions here as well," Sam remarked.

"What happened with Chow?"

"When he found that Wong Wei Yan wanted nothing to do with the illegal businesses, but was himself being used for small illegal businesses, he set out to find the mysterious principal."

"But why did he call the Englishman?"

"Wong Wei Yan had received a few warnings. Since Robert Duncan was the only one he still trusted, he asked him to always follow him and check if anyone else was following him. And so he did. And so it happened that Robert Duncan became aware of Chow. Wong Wei Yan was lured to the house on Queens Road West on a pretext. Duncan followed him and sat down in a restaurant opposite the building. This is where Chow came, who happened to see Wong Wei Yan go into the house and was curious to know what he wanted there.

"When Wong Wei Yan met Dai Lou Chan a few days later, Chow caught Duncan's eye again. After Wong Wei Yan left Dai Lou Chan's restaurant, Duncan set off and followed Chow. The latter noticed and in a small side street in Wan Chai he grabbed Duncan and confronted him. At the time, Chow still thought that Wong Wei Yan was nevertheless involved in the kidnapping of Mui. But it came out that Duncan knew nothing about kidnapping."

"I don't suppose you're suggesting now that Chow had taken the risk of trusting Duncan?"

"Yes, he did, even though he knew it was definitely

not professional behaviour on his part. But there was something that told him that Duncan was telling the truth. He asked Duncan why he was also at the restaurant in the Municipal Centre, and Duncan replied that Wong Wei Yan had been lured there for a reason, which turned out to be false. Chow put one and one together. He knew that we, or Tung, were always being sent pictures and clues. So the suspicion that Mui was being held there was confirmed. Which turned out to be true in the end."

"But why did he have Dai Lou Chan's people helping him with the fictional move?"

"He had once helped one of them as a private detective and from there he asked for this favour."

"Why didn't he contact his brothers from Dai Lou Chan?"

"Well, he had lost the dog, his wife was making his life hell because of it and he didn't want to admit it in front of the others. So he had hired Chow."

The team grinned.

"So he didn't know that the man and the others belonged to Dai Lou Chan?"

"Yes, he did, but he played dumb and the others let him believe it."

"That's crazy. No sensible policeman would do that."

"He may not be a sensible policeman, but he's good."

"He was lucky," cried Keung, "that it went well. It could have turned out very differently!

"There is no doubt about that. But it went well."

"But then, who ordered the murder of Johnny Lee and the hit on Chow if it wasn't Wong Wei Yan?"

"Kwong. He realised that Tung and Chow were getting too close to him. - He was also responsible for the accidental death of Wong Wei Yan's fiancée, Alison Blair."

"Well, Kwong won't hurt anyone else any longer. But what will happen to the Yi Wong now? Wong Wei Yan will have other enemies there."

"We have learnt that some of those who worked with Kwong have fled abroad."

"What role did Dai Lou Chan have in the game?"

"Word had spread that Wong Wei Yan wanted out of the illegal business. But the market did not change. So Dai Lou Chan himself started to find out if it was just a superficial statement by Wong Wei Yan or who else was trying to get rich."

"Sure, what would have been dropped from the Yi Wong would then have been divided and collected among the other syndicates."

"That's how Dai Lou Chan got the idea that it was Kwong. On the evening of 30 June, he called Wong Wei Yan and asked him to come to the restaurant the next evening. But it didn't happen, because Kwong interfered."

"What did he want from Wong Wei Yan?"

"He probably wanted to tell him that it was Kwong and a few others who were still doing illegal business."

"How selfless of him," Mary remarked wryly.

"Inspector Choi will be thrilled that his murder

cases have been solved so quickly."

"Except for the massacre."

"That was Kwong as well. He was so angry when he realised that Mui had been freed that he shot his people. Especially since his people could not give him exact descriptions of the kidnappers. So he suspected that Wong Wei Yan was onto him and would now use this against him."

"Is that why he showed up at his place too?"

"Yes."

"Heavens, this is a mess. What about the Englishman?"

"He will have to stand trial for the murder of Kwong. But otherwise he can't be charged with anything and I think he will get a relatively lenient sentence for this manslaughter."

"And how are Tung and Mui?"

"Mui was kept quiet with sleeping pills. This came out when Tung and Chow freed her and she woke up later. Her grandfather, who is a doctor of traditional Chinese medicine, realised that he had reached his limits here and took her to a clinic in Tsuen Wan. They were able to avert the onset of addiction to the sleeping pills there, but her organs were attacked. It is not yet certain whether they will recover from the constant overdose. But at least there is a possibility."

"Where had Tung hidden them?"

"He had bought a flat in Tin Sum Tsuen a few years ago under a false name. He had put Chow, Mui and the grandparents there."

"And how is Tung?"

"He blames himself. But it's not his fault. He is with her all day. Since he promised not to leave Hong Kong, he was released from custody. At least the charge of four counts of murder was taken off the list. But he still has a lot to face. Chow is not yet under arrest for the time being. It still has to be determined what there is against him. The undercover work as an informant is definitely over."

There was silence in the room. A lot of information had been given. The whole context was confused and the team members felt sorry for Tung, Chow and little Mui.

3 July 2005, 10:06 a.m., Hong Kong Island

When Yan woke up from the coma, he was puzzled. Where was he? What had happened? Why was he in so much pain?

He tried to carefully lift his head to get a better look around. But hammering pain made him give up this attempt quickly. He lay alone in a hospital room. A policeman was standing guard outside the door. He could see this through the glass insert in the door. Yan was connected to the heart-lung machine through a breathing mask. He was on a drip and through the electrodes on his upper body the high-pitched beep of the ECG sounded in rhythm with his heartbeat.

Yan tried to lift his right arm. But apart from severe pain, he had no feeling in his arm. He could not lift it. The duvet was over him. He had been covered up to his shoulders. So he tried to lift his left arm. Here, too, he had pain. But he could lift the arm. With his hand he grasped the breathing mask and slowly pulled it over his forehead. Yan closed his eyes again. He was tired. He wanted to sleep. To escape all the pain.

Gradually, he remembered the surprise Kwong had in store for him.

But then his thoughts drifted into the past. He thought of the best time of his life. When he was still in England. When he was still with Alison. Alison...

Alison opened her eyes. It was early in the morning. The traffic on the street was not yet very loud. Rather, she could hear Yan's light snoring. She smiled. How she loved that sound. Because it meant he was with her. It meant she was not alone. Yan's arm was across her waist. Alison gingerly turned around. Now his forearm was on her stomach. Yan cleared his throat briefly, pulled her closer to him and went back to sleep. Using her shoulder as a pillow. His black hair was rumpled. Alison smiled. She admired him. In everything he did and everything he was. Especially when - as now - he reacted unconsciously. When he wasn't the amorous young man showering her with gifts and love. Gently, she stroked her index finger along his arm, which still lay across her belly. His brown arm that stood out so much against her almost white skin. Alison took a deep breath. He didn't seem to notice. She lifted her hand and ran her slender, long fingers through his hair.

"Mmmmmh..." he grumbled sleepily.

"Good morning."

Tired and rather reluctantly, he opened his eyes and raised his head a little. His face looked scrunched up. He would never understand how one could be so chipper in the early morning and on top of that be so beautiful. A smile flitted across his face. Seeing Alison was the most beautiful thing he could ever imagine. To him, there was no woman more admirable. With her short red hair, pale skin, freckles on her nose and cleavage. He breathed a kiss on her exposed shoulder. How he loved waking up next to Alison.

"Are you awake now?" she asked.

"Hmm." he agreed, still a little tired.

Alison started to laugh. Yan didn't like that at all. Her whole body shook and he had to move away from her a little.

"What is it?"

"You seem like a panda bear to me."

"What? Why?" Now he was awake.

Alison curled up in laughter. Now there was no way he could get a single syllable out of her without her bursting into even more laughter. But he loved her just the same. And he knew that his facial expressions alone only managed to incite her even more. Until, finally, she begged for mercy from her side and slowly, very slowly indeed, calmed down again.

So he sat up, leaned against the footboard and screwed up his face in such a playful disapproving way that tears ran down Alison's face from laughing so hard that she finally grabbed a pillow and held it in front of her face. Yan couldn't help it and started laughing himself.

"Well, wait..." and already he jumped forward to her, snatched the pillow from her and threw himself on her with his whole body. He saw her face - by now bright red - streaming with tears. Her wide, full mouth and her grey eyes glittering at him like diamonds. She tried to push him down, but he grabbed her wrists and pushed them over her head onto the mattress. his body weight made it harder for her to breathe, she slowly calmed down. But not without getting new little fits of laughter again and again.

"Will you calm down now?"

"Yes."

She grinned broadly at him. No, that didn't really look like a 'calmed down' Alison.

Yan tightened his grip on her wrists and looked her firmly in the eyes. In his eyes, Alison could see how much he desired her.

Alison suddenly looked at him with a different gaze. Calm, level-headed, questioning. Probably even a little uncertain, which he didn't know about her. At least not until now.

"I wish we had weekends every day." he murmured to her.

"Why?"

"Because then we could always be together. Because then I could wake up next to you every morning."

"Are you sure?"

He pressed a gentle kiss to her forehead.

Alison turned her face away. She drew her eyebrows together slightly. What was that frown about? Yan became uncertain.

"What is it?"

Now he saw a small tear fall from her eye.

"Alison!"

Yan climbed down from her. He sat up. Alison took the pillow, put it against the wall and leaned against it.

"What's wrong?"

"Do you love me?"

Yan looked at her in amazement. Didn't he show her every day?

"Of course."

"But you've never said it before."

"Alison, what's wrong?"

"You've never said it before," Alison insisted.

"Am I not showing it clearly enough? Alison, you are my everything. The world is not complete until I have you near me, until I can see you."

"Do you love me?"

"Yes, I love you!" Yan had said these words slightly irritably. But all at once he became calm. For the first time in his life he had uttered these words. And therein lay all his happiness.

"Yan..." Alison looked up at the ceiling. How was she going to tell him?

Fear crept up inside him. Was she going to leave him? Was she going to break up with him? The world wouldn't be the same without Alison. He wouldn't be the same without Alison....

"I'm having a baby."

Bang. That was it. Yan stared at her with wide eyes.

A child? Alison was expecting a child? Confused and completely overwhelmed, he leaned back against the footboard. He stroked his hair. A child? With Alison? That would mean... that would mean... that his greatest wish would come true. A family of his own with Alison. A life with Alison.

A broad smile appeared on Yan's face, his eyes began to shine.

"A child?"

Alison nodded. The joy she could now read in his face astonished her somewhat. Was he really happy? Even though she had wanted it to be the same, she was still unsure.

Yan slowly crawled over to her. As if hypnotised, he stared at her still flat belly.

"We're having a baby?"

Alison stroked his head.

"Yes. We're having a baby."

Gently, as if her skin were the membrane of a soap bubble, he touched her belly with his fingertips. In it was his child now? In it now lay his future?

As much as he tried to fight it, he couldn't. Tears rolled down his face as he looked her in the face.

"I wish for a daughter." he said quietly to himself.

"Really?"

He nodded.

"Yes, a daughter. So I can have two Alisons around."

Alison was so relieved that she started to cry. Yan moved closer to her. He took her face in his hands, held her head up. He didn't know if he was crying or laughing, but he knew he loved her.

"Will you marry me, Alison Blair?"

Alison wrapped her arms around his neck.

"Yes. I do."

A doctor entered the sickroom. Yan opened his eyes. The doctor smiled at him.

"How are you?"

"I have a lot of pain. And I can't lift my right arm."

The doctor took the chart.

"No wonder. You barely escaped with your life, Mr Wong. Unfortunately, we had to amputate the right arm."

Yan groaned. The doctor now looked at the equipment.

"I'll give you something for the pain. Then you'll soon feel better," the doctor said kindly.

"That would be great."

The doctor injected a solution into the tube of the infusion.

"Don't worry, Mr Wong. You'll feel much better in a minute. I'll check back later."

"Thank you."

"Goodbye."

The doctor left the sickroom. The policeman closed the door behind him.

"See you later, Doctor."

The doctor just raised his hand and waved. He went to the stairwell. Slowly he went down the stairs and left the hospital through a side entrance. He went into the nearby park. Here he stopped at a bush, looked around. There was no one to be seen. He bent down behind the bush and took out a backpack. Then he pulled the mask off his face, took off the doctor's coat and stuffed both into the backpack. Then he lit a cigarette, slung the backpack over his left shoulder and strolled away.

Five minutes after the supposed doctor left Yan,

Yan's body was shaken by terrible spasms. The equipment sounded an alarm. Dr Lee, a colleague and a couple of nurses ran into the hospital room. They tried to help Yan. But it was too late. There was nothing they could do. A minute later, the ECG gave a persistent beep. Yan was dead.

"Oh man, doctor, what the hell did you give him back there?" asked the policeman who had followed into the sickroom.

Dr Lee looked at him uncomprehendingly.

"Excuse me?"

Appendix

Listed police departments

Metropolitan Police Force, London, GB

Development and Analysis Unit	conducts information services and analysis in serious crime, drugs, weapons and organised crime within contained communities, as well as homicides.
Flying Squad Team	is used in commercial robberies involving money transport, banks, betting offices, post offices, jewellers and casinos as well as investigation of human trafficking.

Hong Kong Police Force, Hong Kong SAR

Criminal Intelligence Bureau	analyses criminal activities, societies, organised and serious crime, and collects evidence for coercive measures from mainly operational crime formations.
Forensic Firearms Examination Bureau	evaluates weapons and ammunition, in addition to performing forensic and forensic tasks.
Identification Bureau	tests fingerprints, collects DNA samples and crime scene photography.
Narcotics Bureau	collects information regarding the importation, production and distribution of dangerous drugs. Money laundering and terrorist financing are also investigated.
Organised Crime and Triad Bureau	Investigates complex organised crime and serious (triad) crimes.

Technical terms

Chairman or Dragon Head	One of the designations for the chairperson/head of a triad.
Heroin No. 4	Designation of the processing state of the heroin. This is the usual form distributed on the street.